The Serpent Sea

by

Linda Lehmann Masek

Fireside
PUBLICATIONS
www.FiresidePubs.com

Cover: Art by:

Rick Dziak, OPA
Dziak Gallery
www.dziakgallery.com

Fireside Publications II
13539 SE 87th Circle
Summerfield, FL 34491

www.firesidepubs.com

Printed in the United States of America

ISBN: 978-1-935517-20-7

For additional information about this book, please contact the publisher at:
firesidepubs@comcast.com or

contact the author at:
masekle@windstream.net

To Katie and my dearest Tigger,
My brave little angels.
With Love always!

Acknowledgments

A number of people were essential in the writing and publishing of my fourth book, *The Serpent Sea*.

First my heartfelt thanks to my mother, Eva Masek, for her proofreading of all of my books, magazine articles and my newspaper column. Her corrections have made me look good for years!

The Reference Staff of the Brecksville Branch of the Cuyahoga County Public Library System were invaluable for their aid with "computer matters" and my constant reference questions, as were the Twinsburg Public Library and the Nordonia Hills Branch of the Akron Public Library System.

To Roberta Wolfer, "friend extraordinaire" at the Cleveland Public Library for many years during my employment there, and to Kathleen O'Driscoll during my years of summer employment at the Western Electric Company in Solon.

I will be forever indebted to Marcella (Marcie) Anderson, my creative writing teacher and her help with the early drafts of *The Serpent Sea* plus her invaluable assistance regarding publishing 'how-tos'. *Marcie, I think of you every time I write.*

Thanks to Dr. William Shorrock, head of the history department at Cleveland State University and his classes in doing the research necessary for all of my books and also to my professors at Case-Western Reserve University.

I'm grateful to my grandparents, Jesse and Hulda Lehman and my neighbors and friends in Northfield and the surrounding northern Ohio area, for their kindness and support of my projects, writing, finding homes for animals, and others – also to the Ohio Telecom Pioneers of the AT&T Company for their words of encouragement.

I am so very grateful to Rick Dziak, OPA of Dziak Gallery in Marblehead, Ohio for allowing the use of an image of his painting, *No Swimming,* to be used on the cover of this book. It would have been nearly impossible to find a picture to more accurately depict the setting of *The Serpent Sea* than this scene. "Thank you, Rick!"

"Thank you" to my publishers and editors at Fireside Publications, Dr. Joan West and Dr. Lois Bennett, for their help and guidance in the preparation of my manuscript.

Lastly to my four kitty "children" who are a constant source of encouragement, imagination, and inspiration as they watch me hovering over my computer. *My Angels*! *I couldn't do it without you!*

Prologue

Key West, Florida

"If once a man indulges himself in murder," – Murder Considered as One of the Fine Arts (Thomas De Quincey)

She was drowning, as the swarthy swirl of foam closed over her head, cutting off the air supply and knocking the regulator from her mouth. Anne Gordon's thoughts returned to the start of a glorious day as she and her twin brother, Edward, had left the dock to go scuba diving in the warm waters off their home at Islamorada. As Anne choked and swallowed sea water, she could see Edward beckoning to her up ahead before the rip current from the mouth of the cave they had been exploring caught hold of both, separating the twins and spiraling Anne head-over-heels back down the long corridor of the underground cavern. She gasped, as the salty sea water poured down her throat – her enemy, this serpent sea, before the cresting wave had vomited her back onto the shore, leaving no trace of her twin brother in its wake.

Unexpectedly, another face swam in and out of her vision as she lay weak and shivering on the shore, the darkly accusing face of her grandfather.

"Why did you leave him to die, Anne? Edward was your twin brother. How could you just abandon him?"

Behind her grandfather, Anne saw a third figure, garbed in black, her long bony neck distended, her lips pulled back in a rectus of a smile – Maud Gordon, her aunt. But she wavered in and out of Anne's mind before finally fading from sight, taking the accusations with her.

"I didn't leave him!" Anne heard her own voice playing back in her head. "I would never have left him to die."

Suddenly, she had been transported back into the cave with Edward, the blackened devil's mouth of the obscene hole in front of her before the freak current had struck them both. As the water filled her diving mask and she began choking and gasping once more, Anne opened her eyes and sat up.

Her eyes finally focused on the lamp beside her bed – her bed in the apartment at Cedar Key. The nightmare faded.

Anne turned on the light with shaking hands; would she ever be free of the guilt hanging over her from that day? Her eyes filled with tears, and she slowly shook her head. The answer came unbidden to her mind; still, after five years that answer was the same.

"Never!"

Chapter One

Cedar Key, Florida

"I remember, I remember the house where I was born."

(Thomas Hood)

"What's a seven letter word that ends in E and means darkly mysterious?" Cristel Slivka asked, her silvery blonde head bent over the evening's crossword puzzle.

"Huh?" Anne Gordon looked across the room, away from the piece of paper she held in her hand.

"A seven...weren't you listening at all? What's in that letter, anyway? You've been twenty-thousand miles distant ever since you started reading it."

Anne got up quickly and wandered over to the window. It was a grim, morosely cloudy sort of day off Cedar Key on Florida's West Coast. Cobweb-like strands of fog shrouded the Gulf, making it invisible.

"Not twenty-thousand miles – just five hundred or so – in Key West. That letter was about my grandfather, David Gordon."

Cristel studied her from under lowered lids over the crossword puzzle. She twisted the glittering opal ring around on her third finger.

"Anything urgent?"

"No. I mean yes." Anne laughed nervously, and automatically reached for the glass of lime juice on the

3

coffee table. As she turned the glass around in her hands, her eyes traveled casually over the apartment she shared with Cristel. It appeared to be an unorganized combination of modern, early American and Spanish furniture, white rattan, dark mahogany and red cherry wood, a veritable hodge-podge, like its owners. But this had been home for the past two years. Her attention returned to the lime juice. Breathing deeply, she tried to steady her nerves before turning to face Cristel's bright, curious stare.

"Yes," Anne repeated more firmly. "It's from my grandfather's lawyer, Ben Caldwell."

"You mean they wrote from New York?" Cristel raised her brows questioningly. "Your mother is in New York City somewhere, isn't she? Just like my family. Is your grandfather there, too?"

Anne sighed deeply.

"No, he's not, although, it's been the family scandal or feud, I should say, for years." She closed her eyes, as Cristel waited quietly, rather like a bird watching for a worm, or in this case, a piece of information. "I'd best tell you the story, at least what I know of it. It was all hush-hush by the time I was born."

Anne twisted the juice glass around in her hand, slopping some of the drink onto the white rattan coffee table.

"My mother, Elizabeth, was born and raised in Key West on an estate called Islamorada. Her father, David Gordon, my grandfather, lined up a local boy for her to marry – someone who would have fit straight into Gordon Industries. He planned for a big church wedding with all the family in attendance. Anyhow, my mother was rather independent and rebellious, a typical nineteen-year old.

At the party where she was supposed to meet her prospective, approved suitor and make a good impression, she stuffed herself on food from the buffet and got blindingly sick to her stomach. She staggered out of the estate onto the main road going into Key West, sat down, and proceeded to vomit up her lunch. Along came a charming, attractive and oh so sympathetic man. He had traveled from New York on business."

"After holding Mother's hand for a couple of hours, she really felt better and took a good look at him."

Anne grinned suddenly.

"Mother liked what she saw. Two weeks later, they ran off and got married. His name was Devon Sharp."

Cristel stirred and drew her legs up under her.

"Your father?"

Anne nodded slowly.

"Grandfather was furious, of course. He took it very personally that his daughter had had the gall to dismiss all of the chosen candidates for her hand in marriage and choose an outsider – a nobody, and a Northerner, to boot! Besides embarrassing the family and disgracing the Gordon name by getting sick in a ditch alongside the main road leading into Key West."

Anne's mouth twisted wryly.

"My grandfather is big on not disgracing the name Gordon. My mother tried to smooth it over. The final straw, so to speak, was when Grandfather insisted Dad change his name from Sharp to Gordon."

Cristel grinned slyly.

"As Marlowe said, 'Man hath no fury when deprived of his rightful name!'"

Anne frowned, stopped her narration and squinted at Cristel.

Her friend's green eyes flashed wickedly.

"You made that up! I don't think anyone ever said that, Marlowe included!"

"Oh, but Anne! He could have! None of those early writers had biographers standing or sitting at their elbow except Boswell and Johnson. I'd be willing to bet even Boswell could hardly put down every syllable by hand!"

"Without a recorder or a computer, likely not."

"Boswell had a big nose, though. I remember from Lit Class." Cristel scrunched down more comfortably in her chair. "So there was a gigantic break-up?"

"Gigantic was a minor word. Mother got cut off without a cent. Even after my father died, she wouldn't go back. But my twin brother, Edward, and I used to go to Islamorada once school was out over the summer – until the accident." Anne looked out the window, but her mind roamed far away in a land of swirling, malevolent water and palmetto trees.

"Anne, go on! This sounds like Galsworthy's, *The Forsyth Saga, Part Two Hundred* on cable*!*"

"You're sure I'm not boring you?"

"Do I look it? Continue! Please!"

"Edward and I drove down to Islamorada for the summer. It was our last year before college. Frankly, Edward had always been my grandfather's favorite. He was generous to a fault with him, and Edward used to pass some of the presents on to me. Both he and I loved to dive and scuba and the area is ideal for it." Anne swallowed hard. "There was an accident and Edward didn't come up. His body was never recovered – and I got blamed for the whole thing."

6

Anne looked away, tears shimmering under her eyelids. "My grandfather has never been able to forget – or forgive."

Cristel reached out and put her hand on her friend's arm.

"How unfair! This grandfather of yours sounds like a real b…"

Anne raised her brows.

"Bad person! I'm sure you did what you could to help Edward get out of the cave. It wasn't your fault he ignored you!"

An unexpected shiver ran up Anne's spine. *How did Cristel know he was in a cave?* she wondered, before quickly dismissing the thought as irrelevant.

"It was strange in a way. Edward was such a prankster. I kept expecting him to turn up at any moment – even weeks after the accident. I couldn't believe he wouldn't walk in and yell, 'Surprise!' at all of us, and we could feel like fools for mourning him."

Anne hiccupped loudly.

"Kind of like Mark Twain's Tom Sawyer and Huck Finn parading in at their own funeral. But it never happened, of course."

"Your Edward sounds…" Cristel shook her head and stopped at the last second.

"It was just his way. He had the personality so people would forgive him anything – even this."

"I gather the personable Edward didn't ever turn up?"

"No. And I…well, you know what happened. I made a bad marriage and got banished, too."

"Your grandfather sounds rather like a king talking to his lackeys."

7

"That's why I've never spoken about this before." Anne fingered the letter, still in her hand, "Because I've been banished until now."

"What's happened now?"

"My grandfather is sick. This letter is from our family attorney, Ben Caldwell. I may have to go home."

"Oh, no! Anne, you can't leave me in this mess!" Cristel rolled her green eyes and indicated the overhead photography studio in the loft, separated from the apartment by the stairwell. "We've got a show coming up next week. And that jewelry designer with the beard is saying he can't make the display deadline. I planned to fill in with my own work." She got up and began pacing the room.

"It can't be helped. I'll make it up to you, I promise. But if my grandfather is sick enough for Ben Caldwell to write…"

"I know, I know! It's just that you're much more creative than I am! And better with that prima donna, touchy designer, too!"

Anne shifted position on the sofa, her slight body sinking deep into the maroon cushions.

"I'll be back for sure before our gigantic show in mid-July. I promise."

Cristel slithered down on the sofa, her long, muscular legs crooked out at an odd angle only she could achieve. She shoved her horned-rimmed reading glasses back on her nose.

"It'll be okay, Anne – honest. And I'm sorry about everything that's happened to you." She bit her lower lip. "I can understand, and I'll manage the photography shop and the artists for a few weeks, easy. I've always been the one who's missing work, gone for days traveling about drumming up business. You have been doing more than your share, ever since…" she stopped awkwardly.

"Since the divorce. Take it easy, best friend. It's not a taboo subject. Lots of people get married and afterward have second thoughts – fifty-two percent of the population, as of the last count. My marriage just didn't work out between us. My typical run of bad luck, I guess." Although it was hardly an adequate explanation for the dismal failure of her relationship with her ex-husband, it seemed to satisfy Cristel.

"Have you heard from Leigh at all?" The other woman twisted the large, silver-engraved opal ring nervously around on her third finger.

"No," Anne answered shortly, "and I don't want to, either."

"I'm not surprised it didn't work, you know. He's different. I mean…I'm not quite sure what I mean."

"Leigh is an actor, first of all, with outside interests. A lot of them."

"His latest interest is called Deidre or Debbie someone. I heard about her from the regulars at the health club in Orlando. It's amazing what people talk about between swimming laps and diving in the pool. She's in movies, too, and happens to be loaded."

"If he marries her, it will be one problem Leigh will have successfully solved." Anne's mouth curved into a hard, little smile as she added, "Everything's ironic in a way. I mean, Leigh married me because of the estate and my grandfather's money. But Grandfather turned around and cut me off completely because of Edward, and because he detested Leigh – claimed he was a fortune hunter. It's the only thing my grandfather and Maud have agreed on in years. They'll both be delighted to hear that we've broken up."

Cristel roused herself enough to ask, "Who's Maud?"

"My aunt. She stays at Islamorada and runs the house. Ever since Edward died…"

Anne wasn't aware of any change in her voice, but Cristel leaned over, patting her hand.

"Don't think about it now. He's gone, and it's finished. It's been over for years."

"If only it were."

Cristel glanced up, surprised at her vehemence.

"Edward was always Grandfather's favorite, like I said. He doted on him. My twin." Anne sighed wearily. "That's why my grandfather blamed me for what happened. I should have known Edward was in trouble that day. I should have tried to get to him earlier. I should have worked harder to rescue him. The situation after Edward died was one of the reasons I decided to marry Leigh. I felt so lost, shut out. Edward had always protected me, run interference, been my own private guardian angel. I'd gone back to New York to my mother's apartment, but I couldn't forget what had happened. Everything just seemed to go sour."

"Don't dwell on it. Your grandfather may feel differently, especially if he's sick. He may be more forgiving and generous. And you'll surely want to visit him before he…"

"Dies?" Anne put in bluntly as Cristel paused delicately. She drew her short legs up onto the sofa. "Yes. I suppose I would want to see him again." Anne paused to catch her breath. "You're a good friend, Cristel. Almost like a sister. And you may be right."

10

"There you are, then." Cristel smiled, and picked up the newspaper. "Now a seven letter word…"

"Macabre," Anne spoke up. Over Cristel's murmur of thanks, she moved to the telephone to talk to Ben Caldwell about when she would be arriving in Key West.

>>>>*Gordon*<<<<

The sun filtered through the white louvered shutters, spilling beams of light across the two men sitting in the room beyond. It was late afternoon, mid-week, and the Miami-Dade Police Department bustled with the sense of urgency common to law enforcement agencies throughout the world.

Alex Stryker studied the man sitting across from him. His superior, Captain Ed Lewis, had been studying the report which sprawled across his desk. Stryker frowned. He had no idea what this was all about; he'd been summoned, no literally removed, from his current case, tracing a ring of drug smugglers who were operating south of Miami.

Lewis stopped shuffling the papers and studied Stryker. The tall, dark haired police lieutenant, his second-in-command, had dressed casually in jeans and a dark-green pullover. Cool gray eyes watched him, analyzing, always thinking; *Stryker would be thinking with a bullet in him or on his way to the electric chair, trying to get around an impossible situation by exploring all the possibilities.*

Lewis knew that Stryker was a bulldog of a force, the type of man who just wouldn't quit once he had gotten hold of something. Ruggedly handsome, the police lieutenant had women swooning over him and never lacked for female companionship.

11

"You're probably wondering why I pulled you off your current case. But we have a situation developing off the coast of Key West, on a dive operation run by Roger Devlin. Maybe you've heard of him – with your background in scuba and all?"

"Sure. Everyone has heard of Devlin. He runs one of the most profitable salvage businesses in the country – hauled up millions from the ocean floor."

"Well, Devlin is currently involved in salvaging a Spanish ship off the coast of Florida near an estate called Islamorada. A David Gordon, big financier, is one of his backers. Anyway, the trouble started with a series of accidents – little things, notes warning the dive-team away. Plus some sabotage of equipment and what have you."

"Sounds like a prank. Almost something a kid would do."

"It stopped being a prank day before yesterday. An experienced diver got killed. According to the Key West police, the whole incident appeared to be nothing more than a diving accident. But...the officer, Armando Catalano, is a friend of mine. Has a real nose for trouble and didn't like the smell of things. He thinks..." Lewis glanced down at the report on his desk, "that it may have been murder."

"It's a long stretch from accident to murder. Could Officer Catalano find any motive?"

"No. At least not an obvious one. Just the opposite. No one could see any reason why anybody would sabotage an operation that could make a lot of money. So..." Lewis steepled his hands thoughtfully in front of him, "I've decided to send in a man undercover. Devlin will know, of course, but nobody else. I need somebody on that dive boat," Lewis' gaze flickered downward to the papers again, "the *Riga*, who can look around and find out what's going on. And with your background..."

"Of diving reefs all over the world, I would be a good choice," Stryker finished up for him.

"Exactly. Your other case is winding down. I need somebody to get down to Key West and out on that boat now. Find out if it really is just a series of bad luck kind of accidents, or something much more."

"Like murder?'

"Look at it this way, Alex. If it's a false alarm from this Roger Devlin, then you'll have a couple of weeks or so on a gorgeous boat with plenty of sun, free diving, food..."

Alex grinned suddenly. "I get the feeling you think this might be just that – a gigantic false alarm."

"But I can't afford to ignore Officer Catalano's report – or David Gordon either. A multimillionaire with that much money, if this shouldn't be a false alarm and I do nothing – you can see my problem." Lewis rose from behind his desk.

"Fly down to Key West. Devlin will be expecting you. Investigate and report back to me with what you find. I've rented a private apartment for you to operate from. It could turn into nothing more than some bad luck on the part of Devlin's dive team. In which case, you'll get a month's vacation, all expenses paid, and a gorgeous apartment in one of the most glamorous places on the face of the earth. And if it should be murder..."

"Right. I'll keep you posted. And send back any other information that I find."

The two men shook hands before Alex Stryker returned to his apartment to start packing.

13

Chapter Two

"The descent to Hades is the same from every place."
                              DiogenesLaertius (Anaxagoras)

The following day Anne drove south from Miami, following Route 1 as it led out onto the Keys. After passing Key Largo of Humphrey Bogart-Lauren Bacall fame, the narrow highway seemed to stretch itself across the water. Built on a small oasis of land, a sun splashed sea surrounded the road on both sides, a sea whose color changed from a transparent emerald green to a smoldering, soul-deep turquoise. Anne stopped her Volkswagen often, pulling off onto the shoulder to gaze, first at the ocean and afterward at the land surrounding it. She lost count of the birds; dozens of ibis and egrets, their delicate plaster-white bodies looking like they had been carved from scrimshaw. Once, she glimpsed a flash of pink and crimson overhead, as a laureate spoonbill dived down toward the waves, snatched a speckled fish from the water and flapped off into the distance.

She drove slowly, savoring the salty smell of the sea and the animal life around her. Anne watched hopefully for a sign of the dog-sized Key deer. At one time these gentle, harmless creatures had been hunted mercilessly and had almost become as extinct as the dodo bird; now, thanks to new conservation laws, they remained safe from extermination. Today the deer all seemed to be in hiding, away from the early heat of the morning.

14

The Keys had changed; more stores, more restaurants, and more tourist attractions dotted the land, as well as a new Undersea Park and a Shark Institute. Where pirates like Teach and Lafitte had once roamed, hundreds of small boats pirouetted on the ocean.

A lighthouse rose on the other side of the last bridge, like a white magician's wand reaching high into the air. The town of Key West resembled a New England fishing village far more than a southern seaport. The area flourished on the tales of yesteryear that told of wreckers, those pirates of the reef who had practiced their lucrative trade and made many a ship end her voyage piled high and dry on the shore, to be ransacked by the local citizens. This tropical seaport with its varied people, so alike and yet so different, had managed to blend into a united whole. It was a world of bright light and soft shadow, where Edward Gordon had drowned five years before.

Anne continued through the town, passing the home of the late Ernest Hemingway; characteristically, a tour bus had parked outside. A "conch" train with its noisy load of tourists came down the street, full despite the intensive heat of mid-afternoon. The gate house of Islamorada appeared farther on, past a final sharp corner.

She'd come home! The road twisted and turned through the heavy shrubbery; flaming red Poinciana, lemon-yellow allemande, and scarlet poinsettia plants the size of small trees seemed to flower everywhere. Their smell filled the air with a cloying sweetness that hovered in the air. Anne cautiously maneuvered the Volkswagen to the brief clearing surrounding the estate. The road continued to wind onward and ended at the Spanish-style colonial mansion. It had been built by her great-

15

grandfather Gordon, with the money he'd made running guns through enemy lines during the Civil War.

She continued past the carefully trimmed shrubbery and up to the veranda. More flowers bloomed here, enormous blood-red camellia bushes and a rare, almost magenta shade of hibiscus, winding its way along a trellis at one corner of the big house, rather like the serpent in the Garden of Eden. Grandfather had added an additional wing onto the west side of the building; a plethora of the brilliantly colored Poinciana had been nourished and cultivated there.

A movement at the far end of the veranda claimed Anne's attention; a man watched her arrival. He stepped back into the shadows before she could get a glimpse of his face. Anne felt a stab of familiarity, but if he didn't want to talk to her… Shrugging, she stopped the car, turned off the motor, and got out.

A second later, the front door opened as though on cue. A well-dressed man, who had always reminded Anne of a young Robert Redford, strode out, hands extended toward her.

"It's so good to see you again! Ben Caldwell told me you'd agreed to come."

"Colin Grant." She smiled her pleasure. Colin had worked for her grandfather for many years, first at the main office of Gordon Industries in New York and later as manager of Islamorada. He didn't look the business type at all – rugged, out-of-doors, he had been the company's trouble-shooter in all parts of the world. From Alaska to South Africa, the name of Colin Grant had been synonymous with David Gordon – and money.

He'd always been calm, patient, and very straightforward, whether deeply involved with top

16

executives of the firm or with his difficult employer. He hadn't changed that much in the five years of her absence except for his eyes. They held a tension about them as they bore into her. Something bothered Colin; Anne would have given a lot in that second to know exactly what that something could be.

"How is my grandfather?" she queried anxiously, wondering if the older man's health had caused the alarm in Colin's eyes.

He sobered instantly.

"He's a sick man – has been for the past two years. But the last couple of weeks – that's why it's so good of you just to drop everything and come. But let's go inside and I can answer all your questions there."

Colin guided her adroitly across the veranda, through the ornate doorway and into the large living room. Anne seated herself on a section of the huge sofa and looked around while studying the room and unleashing memories from her past.

The room appeared exactly the same, a mix of dark mahogany furniture against eggshell-white walls. Louvered shutters hung at the windows, while an expensive Aubusson carpet covered a large portion of the parquet floor. Her grandmother's portrait hung over the fireplace, hazel eyes looking coolly out at the rest of the room.

The tables still held clutter with expensive knick-knacks collected by her grandmother. On a table close at hand roosted two stuffed birds emitting bright splashes of color. Anne recollected feeling sorry for them as a child – sorry that such beautiful creatures had had to die for the purpose of becoming ornaments in someone's house.

A teakwood chest stood close to the doors leading out to the veranda; her grandfather had ordered it shipped home from one of his many excursions to Southeast Asia. Then Colin seated himself on the hard-backed chair across from the fireplace and studied her silently from under lowered brows.

Every piece of furniture stood exactly where it had been when Anne had walked out of the house five years previously. It had never been rearranged; she reflected wryly that nothing short of an earthquake would change the make-up of Gordon Hall.

Colin cleared his throat.

"I was wondering about your husband, Anne. We heard you'd married. He isn't along?"

"We're divorced, Colin. It's been over for a year. I'm part-owner of an art-jewelry-photography gallery on Cedar Key. And I have a partner, now, Cristel Slivka, instead of a husband."

"Ah, well," Colin paused. He seemed to be searching for a change of subject, but then he queried, "What happened – unless you'd rather not talk about it?"

"I'm pretty much over the break-up. I knew it was coming." Anne tried to make her voice sound matter-of-fact which was difficult when she didn't feel matter-of-fact at all. "Let's just say I was alone for a long time before the split actually occurred. Leigh was an actor. We were all right as long as the money held up, but when it didn't..."

Colin patted her shoulder, almost paternally. "I'm sorry – shouldn't have brought it up. Look, just relax and enjoy yourself until I tell David you're here. Go swimming or scuba or something. The reefs are fantastic viewing..."

18

Her face must have changed perceptibly.

"I forgot about Edward. Sorry." Colin rubbed at the sweat which had suddenly appeared on his forehead.

"It's okay. Anne tried to keep her voice steady, and must have succeeded reasonably well. Or possibly Colin wisely looked the other way. "Maybe I'll walk around. Get used to being back again. Do you suppose I'll be able to talk to my grandfather soon?"

"It will be up to Maud. She takes care of him full-time now, and has for months. There was only one instance almost twenty-five years ago when she wasn't at her brother's beck and call. That's the way it's always been. I heard afterward that she'd been ill or something." He frowned. "There have been changes, Anne, in both of them. Your grandfather's had trouble with his eyes. Ever since the stroke, Maud sees for him. She's extremely loyal."

Anne's head jerked erect.

"Stroke? I didn't know he'd had one."

He wouldn't let us call you or your mother in New York. Maud's had her share of problems, too. You knew she had polio as a child. She's suffering from arthritis now. The doctor's prescribing drugs, but it's gotten much worse."

Anne nodded silently.

"All the excitement hasn't helped her either. What with those treasure hunters out on the reef and the movie people in the new wing of Little Isle."

Anne felt her eyes widen. "Movie company? At Islamorada? At the beach house?"

"They came right after the divers discovered the wreck. An old Spanish galleon, the *San Pedro*. Your grandfather became interested and invested in the salvage company. Roger Devlin is the man running the show out there. And some show it is."

"The Roger Devlin? The man who filmed all those television specials on protecting the environment? He's been described as another Jacques Cousteau."

"The same. Anyway, the divers are living out on the salvage vessel, the *Riga*. But one or another is always underfoot, giving daily reports to your grandfather and all."

"My grandfather is good at keeping track of his money. Where do the movie people come in?"

"After Devlin found the *San Pedro* and they began salvage operations, there was a lot of publicity. The next thing we knew Peter James became interested. He's the producer who does all those horror pictures. He called your grandfather, person-to-person, from California, and turned up inside of a week with a writer, Aldridge Thornton, plus a leading lady who is to be the star. Maybe you've heard of her. Diana Moon. And yesterday, Frank Blaine showed up, too."

Anne hadn't heard of Miss Moon, but everyone knew of Frank Blaine.

"The actor? That Frank Blaine?" Anne felt a tingle of excitement go through her. She had enjoyed Frank Blaine for years, first as the star of a submarine adventure series on the television set, and later in the movie theatre, watching the heroic achievements of her idol. And now, according to Colin's report, she would have the opportunity to see Frank Blaine in person at Islamorada!

"The same," Colin said crisply. He scowled darkly for a moment before carefully readjusting his expression.

It went through Anne's mind that her ex-husband, Leigh, had never been one of Frank Blaine's fans, either.

Colin watched her for a second.

"My grandfather seems to have a full house."

"There's nothing new about that." He shifted positions on the sofa before continuing. "Your aunt should be down directly to welcome you."

"I'm down now, Colin, dear." A soft voice spoke up from the doorway. A moment later, Maud Gordon walked into the room.

Perhaps walked wasn't quite the right word. Colin said that both her aunt and grandfather had changed, but he did not say how much. The past five years had been unkind to Maud; she'd aged twenty years at least, or so it seemed. She had always been small and slender, but now she seemed gaunt. Her dark blue dress only accentuated her pallor and brought out the dark lines around her green eyes, which seemed to take up her whole face. Her hair, once such a lovely sunshine blonde settled into a dull, morose gray. Anne remembered that Maud had walked with only the slightest limp; now she could see that her aunt dragged her leg at an odd, uncomfortable angle behind her.

Maud served as a surrogate mother to the twins when they visited at Islamorada over the summer, and blamed Anne the most when Edward died.

"Aunt Maud." Anne concentrated on her face and tried to forget about the unsightly limp as they exchanged greetings.

The older woman held out a cold hand then turned rapidly away to Colin.

The man rose from his chair as Maud came into the room. She wordlessly motioned him back down as she chose a straight-backed chair close to the shuttered windows.

21

Colin cleared his throat. "I've been telling Anne a little about the movie company."

Maud sniffed. Her nose seemed to rise a fraction of an inch into the air.

"Yes, those theatre people. You'll meet them soon enough, I'm sorry to say – at dinner, if not before. Some of them are staying at the beach house – at Little Isle."

Anne almost, but not quite, laughed.

"They can't be that bad. Otherwise my grandfather would hardly have invited them here in the first place."

"Let me tell you, if it weren't for David – I'd send the lot of them packing so fast – but he dotes on that wreck. If he was younger, and in better health, he'd probably be down there, snorkeling or whatever it is that they do. As things are, I have to put up with those divers traipsing in here dripping water all over the floors." She wiped her hands fastidiously on a tiny linen handkerchief that magically appeared from somewhere on her person. The large bloodstone ring she wore on her third finger winked on and off, like an evil eye, flame colored in the light.

"I'm sure Mr. Devlin is doing the best job he can, under the sea and above," Colin put in gently. The man had a reputation for providing a buffer zone in any argument; he seemed to be living up to it now.

"And the wreck likely provides my grandfather with outside interests," Anne added for good measure.

Maud looked down, her eyes hidden. But she responded naturally enough. "You may not be able to see David until tomorrow. Mr. Caldwell is coming out, too." She sat back, waiting for a reaction.

"Ben Caldwell?' Anne tried to keep a level voice, but in reality, she found the presence of her grandfather's lawyer unnerving.

Anne looked from Maud to Colin and back again, sensing a puzzling undercurrent. Quite suddenly, she had to get out of the room.

"Since Grandfather can't see me right away anyhow, I'll look around a bit – think about old times." Anne rose and wandered toward the veranda door trying to be casual, and stared for a moment over the well-tended lawns and flowers of Islamorada. A southeasterly breeze fanned the row of cypress trees down by the wharf, while the waves raced onto the shore, spraying the beach with long fingers of lacy-white rivulets of foam. Turning, Anne was surprised at the look of anxiety on her aunt's face.

"Don't look so upset. I won't stray that far. Not now – just through the gardens and down the beach a ways."

Maud's voice rose. "You must be careful! And stay away from the reef. It can be dangerous. Isn't that right, Colin?" She glared at him, as though daring the man to disagree with her.

Colin spoke quietly. "She's already said she doesn't want to go out and…"

Anne cut in before he had time to finish. Her voice sounded a bit harsh, but she'd stopped caring.

"I haven't been diving since I left Islamorada. Since – five years ago. And I don't plan to go out now!"

"I'm sure you'd like to look around anyway." Colin ignored the interruption as though it hadn't happened, once more acting the part of the buffer.

"Of course," Maud added. "I've put you in your old room."

"That was most kind." Anne smiled, but the strange feeling of unease increased. Colin rose and with a goodbye wave, eased himself out of the door.

"Robin is in the room next door – along with that cat," Maud informed her. "Your cousin has been staying for a few weeks, what with summer vacation and all."

"My cousin? I had no idea she had returned." Anne could feel her spirits begin to lighten. It had been years since she'd seen Robin; they had been good friends once. She would be eighteen now. It would be interesting to observe how the girl might have changed.

"She can hardly wait to see you again. Robin always did rather fancy you, Anne." Maud's voice didn't alter, but it appeared that Robin remained unpopular, at least with her.

"I'll look forward to talking with everyone later."

As Maud started to rise, Anne waved her back.

"It's all right. I know the way."

Anne turned to leave. For the briefest moment, her gaze looked into the mirror on the opposite side of the room. The hatred in Maud's eyes reflected itself in the glass. A moment later and the older woman's expression changed; by the time Anne reached the door of her old room, she'd almost convinced herself that an overactive imagination was at fault – almost, but not quite.

Chapter Three

"The Devil hisself" – (Cristel Slivka)

The room had remained the same, from the Early American furniture to the calico-colored spread neatly folded at the foot of the bed. Everything appeared alike except for the black, short-haired cat with amber-colored eyes, sprawled across the bedspread. She gave Anne a long, measured look, before dropping her head down and going back to sleep. *Robin's kitty*, Anne thought to herself, as she leaned back and shut the door, head pressed against the wall. The last time she'd seen this room had been before her ill-advised marriage to Leigh that changed everything and ended disastrously. Her suitcases stood side-by-side near the closet. Anne saw them as she crossed the room and opened the porch doors wide before stepping out into the dappled sunlight.

She had a clear view of the sea, the waves rocketing up onto the land, spuming frothy lace foam onto the beach. The reef would be out there, too, just under the surface of the water, lurking to catch ships unaware and tear their guts out. From the porch a boat could be seen, presumably the *Riga* and her divers.

Anne's attention turned to the sight of two figures on the sand below – a man and a woman, walking hand-in-hand. As they reached the grass, the woman turned, her long dark hair whipping out behind her; she excitedly gestured with her arm before she turned and ran up the

25

bank, past the boathouse and wharf before disappearing behind the new wing of Gordon Hall.

The man hesitated, as though he planned to follow, but finally moved down toward the wharf. As he ambled along, the sun reflected off the shiny black scuba suit he wore. Anne studied him until he vanished behind the boathouse in the distance.

Frowning, she sat down by the wicker table on the porch. From here, she could see the large, spreading banyan tree, its multitudinous branches supporting the weather-beaten tree house, where the twins had played as children. Staring hard, Anne spotted the four walls high above the ground with a rickety ladder dangling below. Perhaps later, she would go to see it once more, after speaking with her grandfather.

Looking downward again, she noted a group of people crossing the lawn; two men who were trailing the group seemed to be arguing heatedly. The sun glittered on the blonde hair of one woman, shimmering in the afternoon light. This appeared to be the actress Diana Moon. While the man next to her had slightly graying hair at the temples, Anne couldn't see enough of his face to tell if he was Frank Blaine. The fellow glanced up suddenly and spied her enthroned on her chair. As he smiled, Anne had no more doubts. She found herself waving back almost automatically; few women could have resisted the charm of the legendary Mr. Blaine. The movie company had come home to roost for the day, and Anne found herself looking forward to dinner that evening.

She rose and went inside, surveying the bedroom and settling on the night table. There had been a picture of Edward right there, Edward with his gray-green eyes and dark hair, looking straight ahead, so similar in appearance to her own face that it seemed like looking in a mirror. Anne could almost feel the draft of the door opening and Edward marching through, as he had so many times in her past. His voice seemed to echo off the walls in this room.

"*Come on, Annie! Hurry it up. I want to do a number on those guests of Grandfather's. You're slow, and that's a fact!*"

"*A number?*" *his twin muttered, peering under the bed for her other shoe.* "*What do you mean?*"

"*A trick, stupid! Leave your shoes. Go barefoot like me. Otherwise, we won't be in time!*"

"*But what about snakes if we're barefoot?*" *Edward just shook his head and grabbed her arm. She followed him unresistingly out of the room and down the stairs. As they walked through the front hall, he held a finger to his lips and mouthed,* "*They're in the Dead Bird Room!*"

Anne shuddered and nodded in understanding. They skittered to the door and slipped through, going toward the garage in back.

"*You're going to do something!*" *Anne puffed out. She could feel trouble brewing, just by looking at her twin.*

Edward grinned.

"*Let some air out of their tires, that's all!*"

"*Edward!*" *Anne halted, shocked.* "*Suppose we're caught! Just think what will happen!*"

"*You're so timid, Anne! Sometimes I can't believe you're my sister, much less my twin. I won't be caught. There's nobody around to do the catching. Everybody is in the main room, except that toady, Colin Grant. Now come on!*"

Anne followed reluctantly, racking her brain for a way of escape. Edward ran over to the first car and squatted out of sight. She heard the soft hiss of escaping air, accompanied by Edward's soft chuckle.

"Hey, you kids! What are you doing there?"

Anne turned, terrified, like a small animal caught in the headlights of a car. Not so with Edward. He scooted out from behind the Mercedes and shot off toward the wharf. Fortunately, the overweight chauffeur followed, as Edward threw his twin a defiant glance over his shoulder. Meanwhile, Anne sank down on the gravel, too terrified to move, much less run.

Afterward they were punished, of course. But it took Edward no time at all to ingratiate himself again into Grandfather's favor. Her twin frequently laughed about the incident, while his sister merely tried to forget the entire thing.

Anne looked down at her hands to find them shaking uncontrollably. She could hear David Gordon's voice accusing her of deliberately leaving Edward to die that last day in the cave under the reef, of deliberately killing him as her own voice pleaded for forgiveness.

The sharp rapping finally penetrated. How long it had been going on, Anne wouldn't have been able to say. Galvanized into action, she opened the door.

"Gracious, dear, you seemed to take forever. I thought maybe you had fallen asleep." Maud's voice held a trace of exasperation, as if Anne had become one more responsibility she had to see to on the estate. Her aunt peered into the room, saw the cat sprawled on the quilted coverlet, and frowned darkly.

"Sorry, I was thinking." Anne followed her gaze. "I seem to have found a little friend here."

28

"If you wish, I'll chase her out." Maud moved farther inside.

"Oh, no! I like her!"

"You always did like dirty stray children and homeless animals – the underlings of society." Maud made the revelation sound like a fault. "Anyway, I've told David that you arrived. It seems he wants to see you immediately, before Mr. Caldwell gets here tomorrow."

Maud crossed the heavily-carpeted hall and scratched lightly on the carved door before opening it. As they walked in, Anne heard a voice; her ears traced the sound to a cassette player in the corner. She paused, listening; the cassette was Charles Dickens' *A Tale of Two Cities.* Anne shut the door and glanced around the room. There was an antique gold rug on the floor that matched the golden draperies at the windows, and complemented the rosewood bed and table alongside it. Two chairs next to the fireplace, made of satiny teakwood, had been upholstered in blue velvet and trimmed with gold piping, while a Burgess Secretary, constructed of mahogany and inlaid with zebrawood stood by the far wall. A portrait of Washington by Peale hung over the fireplace; it had always been one of David Gordon's favorites.

Anne moved toward the man in the bed and ended by staring at him in consternation. All the way home, she'd been drawing mental images of her grandfather based on visions of five years ago – a stout, robust man, who had known what he wanted out of life and forged ahead to get it. Looking down now, on the waxed remains in the bed, it appeared certain to her that he did not have much time left.

Suddenly, his blue eyes opened. He squinted as he looked up and his expression softened.

"Turn the blasted machine off, Maud. I'm tired of that fool Dickens talking about it being the best of times and the worst of times. I'm sure the rotten economy isn't any better now than it was then!"

Maud hobbled around as Anne spoke up.

"Let me. I'll be glad to turn it off."

"No! Come closer so I can really see you!" As her grandfather peered up, his granddaughter was dimly conscious of Maud mumbling something and leaving.

Anne's attention never wavered from her grandfather's face.

Unwanted tears began to creep into her eyes. Colin said David Gordon had been ill, but hadn't mentioned how sick he actually was.

"I had to see you – to talk to you once more," he whispered.

Anne seated herself on the edge of the bed. His hand was still clasped around her wrist.

"Why didn't you call me sooner? I would have come."

"The sin of pride, I suppose – the Gordon pride. After you'd married and I'd said I never wanted to see either of you again…"

"That's all over. My marriage to Leigh ended two years ago. You were right about him." A bitter smile tugged at the corner of her mouth. "When the money ran out, he just left me for somebody else."

"I'm sorry. I never wanted you to be so unhappy. I drove you to it, into marrying him, I mean." She opened her mouth to object as he continued. "No, it's true. I did force you to leave. After Edward died, we both said and

30

thought a lot of things that weren't so. You ran back to your mother in New York." His mouth turned down. "And I finally realized Edward's death wasn't your fault, and I had to straighten it out before…"

"But you'll be here for years, yet. I'm glad you called me to Islamorada. It can be just like it used to be! I can stay and…"

He relaxed and lay back on the bed, letting go of her arm. "Anne, it's late – almost too late. I can't cheat the grim reaper forever and I know it. Although according to that nincompoop Robert Browning, death is 'the best and the last' fight I'll ever have. How he would know since he was alive when he wrote *Prospice* I'll never understand. Regardless, I've decided to change my will. Ben Caldwell is coming tomorrow. I know he's kept in touch with you. I told him to."

Anne gave a half-sob and reached for the Kleenex box at the side of the bed. She slowly wiped her eyes before responding.

"Your lawyer? But why?"

"Now don't go all driveling on me. I'm doing what I should have done a long time ago – making you my heir. Maud will be provided for, and in case of your death, she will inherit the estate. Of course, Robin will be taken care of, too. But you'll inherit Islamorada and the money along with it."

"No, you can't!"

"Who else do I have to leave it to? You're the only logical person. Besides, call me a selfish, lonely old man, but I'd like you to stay here – permanently – carry on the Gordon tradition, so to speak. And to run the estate when I'm gone…"

"But Mother…"

31

"Despises me! And always will. Can't forgive or forget, I guess. Although, she does have a reason – and she learned it from me, so I really can't complain."

"But she would come!"

He grimaced. It turned into a rictus of a smile.

"No, she wouldn't. Said she doesn't want my filthy lucre. Fifty million dollars. And she turned it down! It and me. But that doesn't matter now. You're here. You came back." He paused and then continued bluntly, "When I die.."

"Not for a long time yet, Grandfather." Anne bent and kissed his cheek; he closed his eyes, his breathing harsh and stertorous. She remained seated there until the even rise and fall of his chest indicated sleep. Turning, she crept mouse-like from the room.

Maud was waiting in the hallway.

"Shouldn't he be in the hospital?"

She sighed wearily.

"I tried. We all did. But you know how he feels about doctors. He wouldn't even allow a nurse! No, he wants to die in his bed, he says. In his own room, at Islamorada."

All of a sudden, Anne felt cold, in spite of the excessive heat. "Isn't there anything they can do? Anything at all?"

"He had one stroke four years ago. The doctors told him then to quit working, but he wouldn't do it. Six months after, he had a second stroke. Only this time his eyesight began to be affected, too. He's been getting steadily worse ever since."

She turned.

"You'll want to talk with Ben Caldwell tomorrow." It was a statement and not a question.

32

Anne nodded confirmation of the fact and then continued. "I was thinking, maybe I'll walk around the estate until dinner. It's a few hours yet."

"You will be cautious."

Anne pulled up sharply.

"Certainly, Maud. I'm generally very careful. Is there any particular reason why I should be more so?"

Maud's fingers twisted at the blood red ring on her hand. "No, of course not."

"Fine. I'll see you at dinner." Anne had an immediate desire to get out of Gordon Hall, to leave behind the tension and oppression that were so stifling. It felt like a weight, an albatross, had been hung around her neck and she desired nothing so much as to shake it off.

Her aunt dropped her gaze to the floor, but the girl could feel her watching, always watching, as she crossed the hall and walked down the stairs. Maud's eyes continued to follow the younger woman until she disappeared into the dense zigzag of shrubbery surrounding the estate before she turned back to care for her brother.

Chapter Four

"By the pricking of my thumbs,
Something wicked this way comes."
Macbeth (Shakespeare)

The air blew in from the sea, a sharp, refreshing blast while the milky-white wavelets continued to splash up onto the beach. Anne stood for a moment staring at the salty ocean and began to feel much better.

Perhaps it was almost subconscious, but she finally moved in the direction of the tree house. Anne ran down the veranda steps and past the extensively trimmed lawn with its multitude of blood-red hydrangeas and rhododendrons, so large as to resemble trees rather than bushes. Reaching the end of the grass, she plunged into the shadow of the woods.

It had turned cooler and the ground was wet and slightly swampy. Ferns seemed to be everywhere, reaching out with their long, lacy tendrils and brushing across her arms, while small-sized palmettos occupied the area the ferns had managed to miss. Overhead, a combination of pine and cypress with trailing Spanish moss closed in on all four sides, obscuring the sky above. Sunlight filtered down through the branches, making speckled patterns on the ground, but as the trees thickened, even this light was blocked out, leaving her alone in the semi-darkness.

Anne tramped steadily on the overgrown path. Every so often she saw the wild poinsettia plants with blooms scarlet in the half-light; they smelled sickly sweet alongside the musty, decayed odor of vegetation. Anne wrinkled her nose at the stench. Several of the palm trees were down and farther along a paurotis tree sprawled with out-stretched limbs directly ahead. She clambered over, scraping her legs in the bargain. The woods seemed absolutely still in that moment. Then she heard a rustling in the undergrowth ahead. Halting, her eyes searched the greenery; she saw a little, black-masked face peering up solemnly. Gasping, the girl held out a hand, but the raccoon, after giving a sniff, turned and ambled out of sight.

Hurrying on, Anne felt suddenly anxious to reach her destination, almost running into the heavy wooden ladder that had been erected years ago by the old banyan tree. She scurried upward, feeling rather like a chicken going home to roost. Swinging up onto the porch, the girl walked over, yanked at the door, and peered inside, her heels making a clacking sound that reverberated on the hollow wood. The place appeared the same; an uneven floor, chipped painted walls, and old, worn-out furniture that Edward had proudly dragged to their *nest*.

Anne moved through the doorway and pulled open the shutters, letting in more light. It seemed so familiar. She ran her fingers over the wooden cabinet in the corner; it felt smooth to her touch and she noticed no dust. The wind gusted through the trees outside causing an unnaturally loud creak. In that instant, Anne sensed that she was not alone.

Someone watched her every move. Angrily, the girl returned to the porch and looked out into the distance.

35

The wind had stopped; the forest seemed still. Not even the sea could be heard from here. She could hear the rasp of her breathing in a very dry throat.

Anne dragged her gaze from the woods to the sky. Apprehension increased like a tidal wave hitting the shore. A flock of egrets rose like small, white snowflakes, lifting off of a nearby palm and soaring skyward. What had frightened them? She didn't know, and decided not to wait around to find out.

Anne turned to scramble downward, but her attention focused on some palmettos moving slowly back and forth below. The tree house was open, so to speak; anyone would be completely off-balance going down the ladder. Anything might be waiting in the undergrowth below.

Anne spotted another movement out of the corner of her eye. A dim figure detached itself from a tree trunk and hurried away through the brush.

The sight of another person initiated action.

"Hey, wait!"

Anne almost fell in her haste to get back down the ladder, jumping the last couple of feet and hitting the ground hard. She paused, panting, and saw him again as he ran behind the trees. The brush shredded her flesh as she scrambled over the downed trees to follow him.

The man moved toward the ocean but, as the palms surrounded everything like a wall, Anne lost all sense of direction. After flailing hopelessly around then becoming more confused by the minute, she reached a break in the greenery, shouldered through and collided with someone standing on the warm, dry sand. Anne got a glimpse of the sea, before she flew backward and landed with a thud on the ground.

>>>>*Gordon*<<<<

36

He studied her lying there, sprawled out in the sand, her halo of dark hair fanned out behind her rather like a large-sized Japanese fan. The gray-green eyes sparkled with fury and something else, defiance perhaps? Alex Stryker felt a flicker of interest course through him; she was a strikingly attractive woman. But what was she prattling on about?

Stillness reigned for a very long moment. Then Anne sputtered, "Why were you spying on me back at the tree house?"

His dark brows rose a fraction of an inch.

"I beg your pardon?"

"Why were you watching the tree house?"

"I don't have the remotest idea what you're babbling about. I haven't seen any tree house. I've been sitting here, thinking."

He watched her untangle her legs and push herself upward. Alex reached out a helping hand which she ignored and clambered up without his assistance.

"Look, I'm sorry. It's just that I...got caught a little bit off balance. Someone was spying on me in the woods. It was unnerving, that's all. Did you see anyone come this way?"

"Only you, Anne. But I could have missed someone. It's a long stretch of beach with plenty of cover and I've only been here a couple of minutes."

"How did you know my name?"

He could detect the suspicion in her tone.

"Colin Grant told me about you. I'm one of the divers from the *San Pedro*. What are you doing wandering around out here anyway? This is a bad time to be alone." His voice almost made the statement sound like an accusation.

"What do you mean?" She leaned over to brush the sand from her blouse.

"You mean Grant didn't tell you? One of the divers died yesterday from a faulty regulator. I'm the one who replaced him, as a matter-of-fact. Just today."

"Died?" He saw her body stiffen, as though this single second were frozen in time. "You mean he was killed?"

"Nobody knows for sure. The police were around, asking questions. But diving accidents happen. I'm not positive they took it seriously." He turned down the beach and she fell into step beside him; her anxiety over the watcher in the tree house seemed to be temporarily forgotten. "It's not a bright idea to explore alone. I hope you'll consider that in the future."

"But don't divers work in pairs in case of emergency? What happened to his partner?"

"There were supposed to be two of them together, but Tilson, that was his name, got separated somehow under the wreck. Then his breathing apparatus malfunctioned and he couldn't get out to surface. The next thing anyone knew, he was dead."

He saw her swallow hard. Just thinking about being trapped in a dark, underwater hole alone and slowly strangling to death made his own flesh crawl.

"Look, Mr..."

"Stryker. Alex Stryker." He stopped suddenly and shaded his eyes against the bright glare of the sun. "There seems to be quite a group gathered at the end of the wharf. I think we'd better get back fast." His voice remained deliberately calm and matter-of-fact but he noted that this seemed to make her more excited, not less.

Stryker began to run. He shouted over his shoulder, "I think there's been another accident!"

He turned briefly and saw her stumbling after him; her shoes filled rapidly with sand, making walking uncomfortable. Stryker galloped ahead. The sun's white-hot rays scorched everything in sight. He glanced back only once. At the last hundred yards, Anne wheezed to a stop, panting.

Stryker spoke to one of the police officers, standing close by the ambulance. Next to them lay a stretcher with what looked like a body draped in white upon it. Alex could see Colin Grant, plus the blonde woman and her two companions who he'd spotted walking on the beach earlier in the day. Several other members of the group remained close, but he didn't recognize them at all.

Stryker watched Anne approach slowly, as though rationalizing that nothing could be achieved by hurrying. Everyone appeared to be talking at once, but she seemed to have difficulty in comprehending the words, rather like a modern day Tower of Babel. When Anne reached the stretcher, she glanced down at it until the driver and his assistant, at a signal from the police sergeant standing nearby, opened the back door of the ambulance and put the body inside. The assistant muttered something about leaving for the morgue. Then the ambulance pulled across the sand and away. Stryker heard someone ask how it had happened. The response came from Colin Grant. "Cut to pieces by the propeller," he stated succinctly.

Stryker turned suddenly and reached out to her as Anne retched. He watched silently, his eyes dark with sympathy as he saw her run, frantically, back down the white serpentine stretch of beach. He didn't try to follow.

39

Chapter Five

"Oh what a tangled web we weave
When at first we practice to deceive,"
Twelfth Night, (Shakespeare)

Later on the night of the "second" accident, Stryker watched Anne as she stared silently out across the veranda at Gordon Hall. The waves swept onto the beach in front of her while a small black kitty wound herself affectionately around Anne's legs.

He hesitated, and then went over and placed a hand gently on her shoulder.

"You should come and sit down. Let the police get to the bottom of this." His expression softened. Strange, he couldn't remember the last time he had felt so *en rapport* with anyone, almost as though he were living out her pain.

Anne turned suddenly toward him, her eyes wet.

"I feel...so abandoned, so alone." She stepped closer. "It's the same sea, the same star-flecked sky. Yet, it's different. There's been another death, another unexplained incident that created this... I don't know, fear. I can feel the fear!"

"You're not abandoned – or alone. And you don't have to be afraid. Ever. Not as long as I'm living and breathing." Stryker fought the impulse to take her into his arms. After all, they had just met – what? – three hours ago on the beach?

40

Everyone had moved from the wharf into the main room at Islamorada. Nobody really wanted to stay and talk; yet, leaving would bring the deserter to the group's attention. And quite a group it had turned out to be.

"Come and sit down," Stryker said again, "with me." He resisted another impulse to smooth her silky dark hair back from her forehead before he turned and led Anne inside, to one of the chairs by the fireplace.

"I saw him right before it happened," the young female diver sitting on one of the hard-backed chairs reported for the third time. She had a cherubic-looking face that, at the moment, seemed lined in shock. Her hands twisted a mangled piece of rope, tying one type of knot after another, first a sheep-shank and then a running bowline. The youngest person present, Stryker knew that she was sixteen years of age and had been nicknamed Squirrel by the rest of the dive team because of her tiny size.

"You've said that three times now," Colin Grant put in. "Let's not hear it for the fourth. All right, there's been an accident, but I'm sure the police will get to the core of the matter."

"But where are the police? Shouldn't they be here right now?" a female voice cooed.

Her enormous blue eyes stared wide with anxiety. She looked vaguely familiar. Diana Moon – fashion model turned actress, her face had graced the covers of many a *Cosmopolitan* and *Vogue*. Stryker remembered something he'd read, that Diana Moon had been noted by Hollywood's inner circle as being on a kind of astrology fetish. The details remained vague, try as he might to recollect them.

An older man who had been seated by the fireplace spoke up. He was in his sixties, bald and wore thick-rimmed glasses. His clothes fit him rather like a boat fits into its slip; his crumpled tan suit looked as though it had been slept in for the past month. But the gray, near-sighted eyes behind the glasses were kind.

"I think that the police are questioning Mr. Devlin and that other diver, Jack Cole, I believe the name was."

"But Aldridge," Diana Moon broke in, "I don't understand why they should be interested. After all, the accident took place at sea, not on land."

"I don't understand why they should be interested in anyone living at Gordon Hall, period. But perhaps you can help us with that. You surely must have more information, being out on the dive boat and all." Colin turned to Stryker standing behind Anne. As all eyes focused on him, he felt Anne's hand squeeze his for comfort.

Alex Stryker looked tired. Diana Moon jerked erect and almost licked her lips as he moved away from Anne and sat down in the chair opposite.

Voices rose in an immediate barrage of questions.

"The police, Devlin, and the other divers are still out on the *Riga*, going over the whole dive ship. And they didn't have any leads when I saw them," Stryker stated flatly. His gaze moved from one to another. It seemed as though his eyes lingered unnecessarily on Diana Moon; glancing up sharply, she met his gaze, her own eyes staring long and levelly.

Just what I need, he thought unhappily. A female barracuda stalking me when I may have a murderer to catch! Yet, she might just have some important information and…

Diana Moon hesitated, then slid into the seat directly opposite and smiled sweetly up into Stryker's face.

Anne roused herself and saw the glance between the two; Miss Moon seemed to have an admirer. Looking around, she caught the eye of Squirrel, who watched the ex-model turned actress with a look akin to jealousy in her blue eyes. Then more people joined the group.

One man appeared older with graying hair, but Anne had eyes only for the other – Frank Blaine! Yet, as he leaned against the mantel, this seemed to be an elderly Frank Blaine with none of the usual cake make-up; he looked at least twenty years older than in his last movie. The ageing actor caught her gaze and smiled, radiating confidence that he could still win over any woman in the room. Anne, too, responded automatically, as women had responded to him since the beginning of time. He deliberately walked over from his place by the mantel and took the chair next to her.

Diana Moon continued talking.

"P.J., what is going on out there? What are the police doing?"

Anne stared at the other man and realized he was Peter James, the noted producer. During her ill-fated marriage, Leigh had tried constantly to get a part in one of Peter James' pictures. He had worked to no avail. It seemed that the impeccably-dressed Mr. James was as impossible to contact as the President of the United States.

The elusive producer attempted to answer Diana's question.

"I'm not sure what is happening. They're out on the boat – have been for almost two hours."

43

"I knew this was going to be a bad day when I looked at my horoscope during breakfast. The first Monday in May…"

"Please, Diana! Let's not get started on that," Frank interrupted. "The one thing I don't need is more hocus-pocus about a horoscope! What I want to know is what kind of protection the police are going to provide."

Colin Grant had gone over to the sofa and collapsed as though his legs could no longer support his weight.

Blaine halted his tirade to catch a breath.

Anne was disturbed, thinking that Colin should say something reassuring, despite the fact that nobody seemed remotely reassured about much of anything. But her grandfather's movie deal would evaporate in a short time unless somebody did something.

"I'm positive the police will come through," Anne began.

Someone sniffed behind her.

"But even if they don't, my grandfather will be happy to put on extra security people once we are certain this isn't another accident."

"But Miss Gordon, you can't have any doubts," Peter James interrupted. "Two deaths, in such a short period?"

"Mr. James…"

"Call me P.J.," he instructed.

Anne was spared calling him anything by the arrival of Roger Devlin from the dive boat. He held up a hand to stop the babble of questions that reached him. His eyes found those of Stryker's before he made his statement.

"Yes, the police are still on the *Riga.* They are officially investigating the matter."

Aldridge Thornton looked bewildered.

44

"But why would anyone want to stop work on salvaging the *San Pedro?*"

"That's exactly what we'd all like to know – two deaths, plus all the other little occurrences the last couple of days." Colin Grant's voice mirrored his disgust.

Diana Moon looked at Colin with her soulful eyes.

"Their time had come. As...er...Faulkner said, 'For whom the bell tolled. It tolled for them.'"

"It was Hemingway, Diana. Hemingway!" Peter James snarled at his leading lady. "Don't you ever read anything but movie fan magazines?"

"Actually, I believe it was John Donne who made that rather famous pronouncement. Hemingway borrowed it from him," Aldridge Thornton piped up.

P.J.'s mouth tightened ominously as he glared at the screenwriter.

Diana subsided, her eyes welling with tears.

An embarrassing silence followed the exchange until Anne spoke up.

"You mentioned some occurrences? What sort of occurrences? What else has been happening?"

Roger Devlin stood up suddenly and faced everyone. "Someone went too far with their little tricks this time. I think that one of us here is a murderer!"

The room became very quiet.

Anne glanced into the mirror and caught a glimpse of a figure dressed in black, avidly listening halfway down the stairs. Maud! How long had she been standing there? She wondered if Stryker had seen her aunt. Her gaze returned to him as the man rose suddenly and prowled back and forth in front of the open windows.

Anne's gaze intensified as it followed Stryker's movements; he reminded her of a caged animal waiting to strike. What had been his part in all this? When she found him on the beach, he claimed to know nothing of the person spying in the tree house and possibly for a good reason. If he had rigged the accident at the dive site, he would want to be far enough away to avoid suspicion, and yet near enough to find out if his plan had worked. What better place to loiter than on the beach?

The silence broke when Frank Blaine knocked over his half empty liquor glass. It fell with a crash and splintered on the parquet flooring. Then everyone talked at once.

Anne continued to keep her eyes trained on Alex Stryker. His expression seemed bland as cream, like a self-satisfied cat gloating over heaven knew what as he met her gaze. Suddenly she had a fierce desire to find out exactly where Mr. Stryker had been when the first diver went to his death after leaving the ship *Riga*.

>>>>*Gordon*<<<<

Anne had trouble falling asleep that night. The blood-streaked face of a black-clad figure kept appearing every time she closed her eyes. Finally, daylight appeared in the east and there was a light rap on the door before it swung inward.

Maud! She limped around the corner of the heavy dresser and made her way to the drapes, slowly drawing them back. As the sunlight radiated inward, Anne sat up.

"Sorry to wake you. But it's after ten. Your grandfather is with Ben Caldwell and I thought you would want to know."

Anne jerked erect and rolled out of bed. Feeling slightly irritated, she pulled a terrycloth robe around her shoulders.

"I couldn't sleep. I wanted to see Ben when he first arrived."

"Don't worry. They won't be finished before lunch. You can see Mr. Caldwell since he'll be staying. Your grandfather may be coming down, although with Robin out most of the night with her young man, I don't suppose he'll be in a very good humor."

Anne stopped in the act of pulling on a blouse.

"I didn't know Robin had a young man. Is that why she didn't turn up yesterday evening?"

Maud pursed her lips.

"Right you are. She never came home until after two. Missed all the excitement. Your grandfather is fit to be tied."

"But who is the man? Anyone I might know?"

Maud shrugged.

"One of the divers off the *San Pedro* – Cole, I believe his last name is. He's coming to lunch, too, and bringing a friend – Robin's idea. He wants to meet the rest of the family, it seems."

"My grandfather doesn't approve of Mr. Cole, I gather."

"Not hardly. The idea of your cousin keeping company with a man who doesn't even have a regular job…"

A rugged, dark-haired face appeared unbidden in Anne's mind. She almost felt Stryker's hand on her shoulder again as he attempted to comfort her the night before, warm, firm and safe. Her skin tingled just remembering the feel of his touch.

"He might not be like that, Maud." Anne reached for a comb and began running it absentmindedly through her thick dark hair. "He could turn out to be very nice.

Besides, better Robin meets him here than off somewhere on her own."

Maud gave an unladylike snort and passed through the doorway. She didn't even deign to answer.

Anne carefully made up her face, turned, and left the bedroom. The mahogany door to David Gordon's room remained closed; the lack of light in the hall and on the stairs cast an eerie reflection on the dark-paneled wood. She shivered involuntarily and hurried down the stairs in search of breakfast.

The dining room had been set for lunch; the girl stole guiltily through to the kitchen in back. A white-garbed figure bent over a porcelain dish of cat food on the floor as the black cat wound herself around the woman's legs.

"Why, Miss Anne, is it? Miss Maud said you might be down shortly." She beamed and straightened, a smile creasing her well-worn face. Anne searched for her name and found it.

"It's nice to see you again, Tisha. But I'm sorry to be such a bother. Just coffee will be fine, if there is some. Or tea." Anne slid into a place at the small table next to the stove.

"Miss Anne, have some of these listi. I made them up this morning." She put a breakfast platter down on the table. "The sugar for the leaves of pastry is right here, too. As for being a bother, think nothing of it." Tisha sat down opposite, cramming her large frame into the creaking chair. "What with the goings-on here today, police and everybody…"

Anne stopped with her coffee cup half-way to her lips. "Police? Because of the accident yesterday, you mean?"

"Ah, but it wasn't an accident at all, Miss Anne. At least that is what people say. They think that the diver was pushed under the propeller. But it doesn't matter. They won't catch the murderer. Not a chance. Not with the curse on that wreck!"

As the other woman said the word murderer, Anne choked on a piece of listi.

"They're sure? That's what it is? But why? And what is that you said about a curse?"

Tisha's voice dropped an octave.

"Much as that Mr. Devlin doesn't want to admit it, I could tell him why he'd been having so much trouble raising the treasure from the *San Pedro*. There was a curse put on all that gold by those poor Indians in Mexico or wherever, who mined it. So many of them died in such torment! Suffered because of the Spaniards. So they cursed the gold and the *San Pedro* sank! Now the gold belongs to the sea and the sea will keep it for its own. Mark my words! All his money and fancy equipment isn't going to help that Mr. Devlin at all. Not in the least!" Tisha sat back, her lips forming a complacent smile over her prophecy of doom.

"You know that's ridiculous!" Anne said it far more sharply than she intended. "It's a pack of superstitious nonsense!" She bent to stroke the black cat, which had finished her breakfast and ambled past.

"I agree," said a voice at the back door. "You should know better, spreading such positive rubbish." Anne turned and confronted her cousin, Robin Gordon, for the first time in many years. Robin smiled, pushing her silky dark hair back from a perfectly oval face. "So good to meet you again, Anne. I see you've met my kitty, Jezebella."

"Yes. She was sleeping on my bed when I arrived." Anne studied her cousin from under dark lashes. The poem they had chanted together as children ran through her mind.

March winds will blow and we shall have snow. And what will Robin do then, poor thing?

This Robin had sprouted beautiful feathers and was no longer shy and out in the cold. She wore the traditional garb of the Key West area; white tee-shirt combined with white shorts. The tee-shirt had the words, *Mag-ni-fi-cat* scratched across the front, with a small black cat reminiscent of Jezebella.

Tisha continued talking, filling in the conversation gap, her mind still on the Spanish curse and the San *Pedro*.

"Now Miss Robin, you know it's more than accidents that have been happening out on that boat of theirs – too many strange events that just can't be explained. And another diver has been killed!"

Anne saw the exchange of glances.

Robin turned back to her.

"You must not let Tisha upset you. There have been some small problems out on the dive boat, *Riga,* as Mr. Devlin can tell you."

"I'm positive that Mr. Devlin is competent. But what other things have happened?"

Tisha sniffed.

"Fires starting for no reason, equipment disappearing, not working, or not arriving from Miami after it's been ordered – and the first diver being killed. It's a curse, I tell you!"

"Curse, smirch. It's a mishap. A faulty regulator could cause it to happen to anyone."

Her cousin gave Tisha a cool stare.

"They've been having a little run of bad luck, that's all. But things will get better. You'll see." She smiled her brilliant, flashing smile, showing the perpetual optimism of the young.

Anne gulped down her coffee and stood up.

"Thank you again, Tisha. For everything."

"You just remember what I said, Miss Anne. Be careful if you go out on the boat. Mr. Devlin or no Mr. Devlin. Watch your back, as my elderly mother used to say!"

Anne trailed Robin out of the kitchen with Jezebella scampering at her heels. They all moved down the hall and into the main room of Islamorada, away from the kitchen, before Robin continued speaking.

"'Curses, foiled again!' as they say in the comics. Don't let this rigamarole get to you, Anne. The locals..."She shrugged her shoulders expressively. "Anything for gossip. That's all it is. Besides, it might be a good idea if you did go out to the *Riga*. That way you can see for yourself what kind of an operation Devlin is running. You might even be able to dive. I remember you used to."

"I don't go underwater," Anne responded, perhaps too quickly. "Not since the last time I was out on the Keys. But I'd like to see what they're doing. That is, if it could be arranged."

"Good. I'll talk to Jack and let you know. He's a special friend of mine and I know he'll help – shouldn't be any problem at all."

She linked arms and steered them toward the veranda.

"You might as well know, Jack and I are very close. In an effort to protect his interests, I am supporting the project one hundred percent."

"That shouldn't be hard. It seems like a worthwhile thing to do."

"It is... so much more interesting than being in school. Devlin and his crew started about four months ago. I could hardly wait for college to let out for the summer."

"You did go to Radcliffe, then? How is it?"

"Dull at first. '*Nor iron bars a cage*' as Byron said. I couldn't wait for the term to be over. But things are working out just fine here. I've never felt like this about anyone else before I met Jack."

"But you haven't known him for very long. Not more than a couple of weeks," Anne added delicately.

"You sound just like Grandfather! I know all I need to. That's why I wanted Jack to stay to lunch. If Grandfather comes down and gets to know him a bit better..."

"You could be right. Does Jack feel the same way about you?"

"He's just shy. He sees all this," she waved her arm vaguely in the direction of the lawns, swimming pool and wharf. "Islamorada is intimidating and so is Grandfather. But you'll find out how wonderful Jack is at lunch. Just wait!"

Anne glanced at her. She seemed lit up with enthusiasm and a kind of inner light, eyes bright, lips parted eagerly. Exuberant – along with a kind of quicksilver brightness. Studying her, Anne wondered if she had ever had the same radiant expression. Had she looked like this after first meeting Leigh Giddings?

52

The dinner gong sounded, interrupting the reverie.

"I'm sure you're right." And smiling slightly, she followed Robin into the dining room, leaving Jezebella snoring on one of the priceless Chippendale chairs.

Chapter Six

*"For he on honey-dew hath fed,
And drunk the milk of Paradise."*
Kubla Khan (Coleridge)

Jack Cole brought his friend, Alex Stryker, for lunch at Islamorada. Anne watched quietly as Robin and the two men entered through the alcove leading to the elaborate dining room.

Anne could feel the flush staining her cheeks as she saw Stryker quizzically regarding her; she should have considered the fact that Jack Cole's friend would very possibly be the attractive older diver. Then her attention was claimed by the younger man as Robin linked arms; Anne studied him with piqued interest. He was tall, extremely well-built and resembled a lifeguard Anne had had a crush on while in high school. He said hello and flashed a broad grin; it crossed her mind that he would have done well in an advertisement for toothpaste.

The others filed in. Once they seated themselves, any humorous aspects to the situation faded; the tension in the room remained too acute for anyone to see anything amusing.

The first obvious conclusion concerned Diana Moon; the sultry bombshell from the night before found Stryker more than slightly attractive. She had seated herself down at the far end of the table and, although she seemed to be deep in conversation with her co-star, Frank

54

Blaine, her eyes wandered periodically up toward Stryker's seat across from Anne.

Robin talked constantly. Cole, on her left, smiled nonchalantly through the chowder to the fish course, but Anne, watching under lowered brows, had the feeling his mind wandered elsewhere, perhaps considering the value of the sterling silver on the dinner table?

David Gordon with Maud hanging close by his side like a black attachment, sat at the far end of the table, opposite Diana Moon. Although he remained politely attentive, Anne could see by his slightly flaring nostrils that her grandfather didn't like Robin's friend one little bit. Maud merely turned up her nose and reminded Anne of Mrs. Danvers in DuMaurier's *Rebecca.*

Meanwhile, Peter James, the film's producer, talked quietly to Frank Blaine, leaving Diana Moon on her own. Ben Caldwell, David Gordon's lawyer, saw it too from his position close to Robin.

Anne turned to Aldridge Thornton, who had seated himself on her left. The slightly balding little man seemed to be off in a world of his own and completely ignorant of the overtures going on around him. She wondered if he was happier not realizing what had occurred. Anne leaned over trying to bring Aldridge into the conversation, or at least make an attempt to do so.

"My grandfather mentioned that you're a writer, Mr. Thornton. Have you been out to see the *San Pedro?*"

He half-smiled.

"P.J. and I were out there yesterday on the *Riga.* Fantastic set-up they have. The dive boat can sleep up to fourteen people, you know. That's where Devlin and the other divers are now."

"Really?" Anne murmured politely. She wondered idly how Jack Cole and Alex Stryker had managed to get excused from work for a good part of the day.

"There haven't been any more accidents, have there?" Robin asked quickly. She had been monitoring the conversation from her place at the table.

"No, not a thing. A police officer named Catalano was out this morning. But nobody seems to be able to prove anything about yesterday's, ah..., occurrence." Aldridge paused, leaving everyone with the distinct impression that he had been going to say murder.

Silence ensued for a few moments until the shrimp in some kind of white sauce had been served.

"Do you see yourself writing a script about the *San Pedro*?" Anne finally queried.

"That will depend on P.J. and whether or not he can get financial backing. It might be a good yarn. Look at *Jaws* and the sequels and the kind of business that did years ago. People like a good fish story."

Peter James cut in smoothly; Anne hadn't realized that he had been listening.

"But disaster pictures could be going out of date. *The Deep* wasn't as popular, and that was done only a couple of years later. Now everyone seems to be hooked on science fiction or comic book heroes like Batman or Ironman."

Ben Caldwell, who had been quiet up to this point interjected, *"Jaws II* and *Jaws III* turned into gigantic financial disasters if I remember correctly."

"Just my point," P.J. added. "But I might be tempted to let Aldridge do a script anyway, if it weren't for all of these weird accidents. I've even heard stories of a curse on the gold they are bringing up."

David Gordon snorted and broke his silence for the first time.

"You don't believe that, surely – just a lot of nonsense!"

Anne thought back to the conversation with Tisha in the kitchen earlier. The rumor of a curse seemed to have travelled the length and width of Key West in short order.

"There might be something to this one," Aldridge stated. "I've been doing research on the entire area. It seems that there have been a number of strange occurrences associated with salvage attempts." He speared a piece of shrimp and continued. "Of course, many of the incidents weren't verified. But even so, there have been an unusually large number of serious accidents."

"It's just a lot of rubbish," Jack Cole, Stryker's diving partner, spoke up, the scorn plain in his voice. "Next, somebody will be suggesting we should get Clive Cussler and Dirk Pitt from that movie *Raise the Titanic* in here to do the diving! Nobody could honestly believe that anything happened because of a curse." His eyes passed challengingly from Aldridge to Ben Caldwell.

"You can hardly be too careful," Ben put in sensibly. Since this could not be disputed in the light of two men dying, everyone fell silent.

Trying to keep the conversation from being marooned, Anne turned back to Aldridge Thornton.

"What sort of things have they uncovered at the dive site, then?"

"Gold bars, jewelry, old cannons and such. We've been fortunate to get hold of a manifest list that was originally intended for Phillip II of Spain. It gives a pretty exact description of everything that had been shipped on the *San Pedro*. There's a lot to be recovered."

Sensing interest, Aldridge continued.

"If you'd like to come out to the site of the wreck, I'm sure it could be arranged."

Since this was a confirmation of Robin's invitation, Anne accepted.

"It would be fine. I'll bring my camera and take some pictures."

"You're a professional photographer," Ben added. "Maybe the newspaper would print some shots. It sounds like Devlin could use all of the favorable publicity he can get."

Peter James frowned, but he said, pleasantly enough, "That's a good idea."

Anne had the distinct impression that he normally didn't like any suggestion which wasn't his.

Only hearing the last part of the conversation, Robin questioned.

"What's that about publicity?"

"For the *San Pedro*." Aldridge Thornton sounded more enthusiastic by the minute. "You certainly should have a look at the loot that has been brought up," he added. "I'll speak to Devlin as soon as possible."

Anne opened her mouth to voice a reply, but everyone's attention turned to the head of the table as David Gordon rose, leaning heavily on Maud's arm. In that moment he seemed just what he was, a tired, half-blind, old man. Anne no longer had the feeling of domination and ruthlessness she had associated with him for many years; he looked like he wished nothing more than to be at rest.

While Maud pushed the wheelchair toward the elevator concealed cleverly beyond the staircase, everyone rose up from the table as though on signal and moved out toward the veranda for coffee. As they hovered in a group, Diana reached into her bag for a cigarette and offered them around. As they all lit up, Anne noticed Diana's hand shaking slightly. She tried to stop the movement, but only succeeded in making things worse.

"Is anything wrong?" Anne murmured softly. The answer seemed obvious, but she needed an opening to encourage the actress to confide her troubles.

"Everything! That first diver dying and the accident yesterday! I wish I'd never heard about making this movie! And now there's supposed to be a curse on the *San Pedro*!" She shuddered dramatically and continued. "I'll tell you one thing. This is a bad period for P.J. and I expect anything to happen!"

"Bad period? How do you mean?" Anne queried.

"His horoscope. He's a Gemini! I've cast his horoscope and the alignment of Jupiter and Saturn is disastrous. He is supposed to suffer some major catastrophe before the year is out!"

Anne almost laughed, but stopped in time. Diana seemed serious.

"And you think the catastrophe has to do with the *San Pedro* – concerning the money he's invested in Mr. Devlin's company?"

"But of course! It's plain as day! And I'll tell you something elsc. The murderer," and here she lowered her voice dramatically, "is a Scorpio. I've figured it out. And there are at least three here that I know of!"

Anne started in surprise and then took a drag on her cigarette. Her voice stayed calm.

"You honestly believe that the stars will tell you the murderer?"

"Absolutely!" And Diana indicated the group wandering around on the veranda.

"So all right. Who are the Scorpios in this motley little stage and dive crew?"

"That man who runs the estate for Mr. Gordon. Grant, I think his name is."

"Colin Grant. I've known him for years and I'd as soon suspect myself as him!" Anne paused and hesitated. How sure could she be? What about all those business deals that Colin had conducted for her grandfather? Anne's attention shot back to Diana Moon.

"That lawyer is another. Ben Caldwell. I spoke to him right after dinner and he told me he is a Scorpio!"

"But he wasn't even here at Islamorada!"

"He has the right sign," Diana stated stubbornly. "But I honestly think the best bet is the last."

"Who?" Suddenly Anne had the feeling she already knew as she heard Alex Stryker laugh uneasily from his position behind her.

"Since you brought it up, I'm a Scorpio," he muttered.

"Yes," Diana murmured in a lusty voice. "I knew that. But it couldn't be a strong, handsome man like you." She looked at him with limpid blue eyes and sidled even closer.

Anne watched the little tableau unfolding in front of her. Her own reservations concerning Stryker had been considerable.

Anne had been quiet for too long, but Diana looked only at Stryker with an adoring expression on her face. Then the initiative vanished as a dark-suited figure stopped in front of them. Anne looked up at everyone's favorite leading man, Frank Blaine.

"Has Diana been telling you about some of her horoscope theories?" he said, appearing amused.

"They're not just theories any more, Frank!" Diana spoke sharply, her attention veering away from Stryker. "There is something else, but I'm not sure what, exactly. Just that yesterday, when I was out on the <u>Riga</u>, watching them dive, I could feel someone watching me! It made my skin go cold, I tell you! All those figures dressed exactly the same in those black scuba suits. It reminded me of the devils dancing on Halloween night!"

Anne dropped her eyes, thinking about the time in the tree house. Someone had been watching there, too.

Frank spoke up immediately. "That's nonsense! You have an overactive imagination! Here's Mr. Grant. Surely he can tell you the same as I!"

Considering what Diana had just said about Colin being a major suspect, Anne hardly thought that his appearance right now would be particularly soothing.

Diana tossed her head.

"Sometime I wish you weren't a Capricorn, Frank. You won't get upset about this business until the murderer knocks at your door and sticks a knife into your throat!" She savagely snubbed out her cigarette.

Blaine flushed an odd hue of scarlet and looked like he wanted to wind a rope around Diana's neck and start twisting.

Colin had been hovering in the background during this last exchange; he hastened forward to add his assurance to Frank Blaine's.

Watching the little parody, Anne began to wonder about Diana's fears: *Her face turned up, pathetically appealing, eyes glistening with tears.* Act II, Scene One. *Miss Moon will portray a semi-hysterical woman in fear for her life.* The she chided herself silently. Why would Diana bother putting on an act? Peter James joined the group; he took one look at Diana's tear-splotched face and correctly interpreted the situation.

"Dear, I'm sure there's no danger. Why, I'll even let you talk to Roger Devlin, if it will help."

"Devlin will say anything to keep his precious project afloat," Aldridge Thornton said from across the veranda. He had been standing alone.

Ben Caldwell looked up sharply.

Robin and Jack Cole seemed to have disappeared, at least for the time being.

Diana ignored Aldridge.

"I already have talked to Devlin. And I'm still worried! P.J., you know it's a difficult period for me. Pisces always have trouble at…"

Diana didn't finish her comment about when Pisces always have trouble.

Peter James, giving her a look of complete disgust, turned and walked over to join Aldridge at the bar.

Suddenly, Anne had an idea.

"Look, Diana. Why don't we get a local person out to Islamorada to give us a report? Kind of like an outside consultant – someone who doesn't have any connection with the project or the movie. He could look around the *San Pedro* if it would make you feel better."

Frank Blaine spoke up.

"That sounds like an excellent idea. Did you have anyone in mind, Miss Gordon?"

"Yes, I have. There was a boatman named Saunders. He worked for us a long time ago. I know he was raised in the Keys and is an expert. I'm sure he would be glad to come."

Anne halted, noting Colin regarding her strangely. Then memory returned. Saunders had been the boatman on the day Edward died; he had helped drag Anne up onto the beach after the disaster in the cave.

Colin finally spoke, but he didn't say the expected. "Saunders left our employ a while back. I never heard where he ended up."

"Well, find him!" Frank Blaine ordered from his position at Diana Moon's side. Anne noted that the actress, having played out her big scene for the evening, appeared calmer. She did have to keep in practice.

Colin frowned.

"His brother, Gary, is a tour guide at the Hemingway House in Key West. At least he was the last I heard. I'll check with Maud. She might remember something else about one or the other of them."

Anne's cigarette had burned down to the end.

"I'll be glad to talk to the brother. Maybe he knows where our old boatman is these days." Anne rose, preparing to move back inside.

"An excellent idea. And thank you. I'm sure you'll put Diana's mind at rest." Frank Blaine's famous painted-on smile appeared automatically. For some reason, it didn't move Anne the way it had for years in blackened theatres. Possibly she had seen a little too much of him and his charm lately.

Anne noted that Alex Stryker stayed with Blaine as she turned and walked part-way across the veranda.

Suddenly Diana Moon scurried up.

"I just have to tell you," she murmured, her voice low and throaty, her *Last Night in Lisbon* voice. She

63

glanced apprehensively at Blaine, but he appeared to be studiously staring out at the ebony-black sea. Hurriedly, she turned back.

"I know what you must be thinking. But I am terrified. And that business about a curse! I'm not religious, but…"

"There is no curse, Diana." This curse business had made one too many rounds today. "You can't believe all that gibberish! After all, it is the twenty-first century, not the sixteen hundreds, when they burned witches at the stake!"

"But I do," her eyes widened. "And you will too, when you see the evidence!"

Anne felt a gut-wrenching feeling of fear start to grow inside. *Here it comes. What she's been leading up to all night.*

"You see, there is this light – a light in that old tree house that's back in the woods. I've seen it there, the last two nights – at three-ish or so. And you know who it is?"

Anne wordlessly shook her head.

"The souls," Diana whimpered. "The souls of those poor creatures who died on the *San Pedro*. They've come back to plot revenge. And killing us is how they are going to get it!"

Turning sharply, she scurried mouse-like back to the ever available arms of Frank Blaine, leaving Anne alone with this most startling new development.

Chapter Seven

"The love of money is the root of all evil,"
The Holy Bible, Saint Paul

Anne took advantage of some down time to think about Diana's statement later that evening. The day had passed quietly enough with no interruptions to announce any new incidents near the beach or water. Jack Cole reappeared; he and Robin broadcast their plans for going into town. Ben Caldwell's forlorn expression became a distinct frown as he watched their car pull away; turning briskly, he said goodbye, walked stoically to his red Corvette and drove off. Alex Stryker disappeared. And Islamorada settled down in the simmering heat of the afternoon.

After dinner, David Gordon sat staring into the burnished depths of the fireplace. His eyes told a story of another time and place. When Anne approached and asked if he'd like to join her in a game of chess, the older man nodded.

She found the board and quietly began setting up the pieces.

David's gaze lingered on her before he finally spoke.

"It's good to have you back here. It seems so much longer than five years."

"It was a long time for me, too." Anne led off, moving a white pawn forward on the board.

"So much happened at the very end. Edward died. And you had taken up with that actor fellow." David Gordon moved one of his two black knights, three squares up and over. He seemed to function reasonably well despite his failing vision, through a combination of squinting at the pieces and remembering their positions.

As Anne picked up one of the bishops, she recalled rather irrelevantly, that her grandfather had never managed to recollect Leigh's name.

He glanced up sharply.

"You're honestly through with him for good? No reconciliation in sight?"

"No! No reconciliation." Her fingers closed hard over one of the white knights, nails digging into the ivory piece. Anne carefully placed it on the board and jumped it forward three squares.

"Leigh turned out to be exactly what you claimed – a   fortune hunter, nothing more or less. You were right about him all the way."

"It brought me no joy. You must believe that." Her grandfather swooped down on one of her knights with his rook, capturing it. "Your king is in check." The older man scowled. "I may have been right about your ex-husband, but not about Edward. I realized afterward that you weren't to blame and that you certainly hadn't deliberately killed him. I should have told you at the time. But it seemed that I had to blame someone and it just happened to be you, since you were there. The boy had always been impulsive. What happened was almost inevitable."

"I understand. I did exactly the same when my marriage went under – blamed everyone in sight except myself. So in certain ways we are very alike. But let's forget it." Anne tried to turn her attention back to the game. Her hapless king needed protection. She moved the queen ahead to block.

"After all this time, it seems inadequate to say, 'I'm sorry,' and expect that to cover everything. You asked for my forgiveness five years ago. I give it freely to you now."

He paused.

"You're generous, Granddaughter. And I have been, too."

Anne jerked upright.

"Do you mean you've gone through with it? Changed your will?"

"I always follow up on my ideas. It's the reason I was successful in business for years. Did you think I would stop when dealing with my own family?"

"It wasn't necessary. I didn't want anything. I honestly never expected it of you."

"I haven't much time left. I know that. And I've made you my heir. Islamorada will be yours when I die – along with the money to manage it. And the treasure from the *San Pedro* – that is, if anything is actually salvaged."

Anne chewed on the end of a nail, brows furrowed in thought. This action of her grandfather's would change everything.

"You're a survivor, Anne. And Islamorada was meant to be yours. It belongs to you. Gordon Industries is an enormous responsibility. People will be dependent on you. But it's in your blood. It's a part of you."

"I can't comprehend this. Who else knows?"

"Ben Caldwell and the two of us. That's all."

Anne picked up a rook. She turned it over and over then finally set it down, warily, on the chessboard.

David Gordon watched her with sober eyes, saying nothing.

Anne's heartbeat quieted as she sensed rather than heard a faint movement at the top of the stairs. She had a most uncomfortable feeling that someone else now knew how the will was going to read.

Her grandfather won the chess game of course, faulty vision and all.

>>>>*Gordon*<<<<

Later, Maud came back from somewhere out on the veranda; the older woman seemed to know instinctively when to appear. She wheeled her brother out of the room. Anne watched him go, his papery white face etched with tired hollows.

The air smelled of rain. Anne threw open the doors to the balcony and ambled out; the lower section of the house appeared dark although lights glittered in the west wing. Perhaps Aldridge Thornton worked on his script? Or Frank Blaine romanced Diana Moon? Anne shrugged, thankful that she could remain uninvolved. Puzzled by all that had taken place, she went back inside to bed with Jezebella curled up cozily against her legs.

Sleep did not come easily. Eventually, Anne sat up and turned on the light, deciding there was no point in trying to ignore what bothered her. A ghostly demon needed to be exorcized – a demon named Leigh Giddings.

The first time she laid eyes on him many years ago had been a Wednesday. It was exactly one month after Edward died. Anne had returned to her mother's home in New York in a belated effort to forget her twin's death.

It hadn't worked, but the trip home had seemed a good idea at the time – change of climate and all that.

Anyway, between running to see the Rockettes at Radio City, going to the theatre every night, and shopping most of the day, Anne managed to lose one of her credit cards. It wouldn't have been quite such a disaster if someone else hadn't found it and charged over ten thousand dollars to the account.

So, there she sat, in the credit office of one of the best known stores in the country, when Leigh Giddings walked in. He was in charge of the store's security and needed her statement on a number of forms so that there would be no question of liability.

Somehow between signing the forms and exiting the office, he managed to issue a brunch invitation at the Plaza Hotel. Anne found out that he wanted to be an actor, and the security job filled in temporarily to pay the bills until his first big break.

She should have been more cautious; after all, anyone with unlimited credit could hardly be poor. But all her machinations in and around downtown New York, all her efforts to forget Edward's death, had been in vain, and Leigh seemed a new, desirable interest.

The same could be said of Leigh. Unfortunately, he wanted to find a woman, preferably with cash to her name to pay the bills and allow him to concentrate on his acting career. Into Leigh's life walked Anne Gordon like a gift from heaven.

Needless to say, he turned his charm on full throttle. He seemed to be everything a woman could ever want in a man; handsome, kind and considerate. Anne felt flattered and very fortunate to have discovered him in her time of need.

Anne had always wanted a church wedding, but Leigh claimed he felt overcome with his true love for her and argued successfully for haste. At the end of the week, they married quickly in front of the Justice of the Peace; Leigh flew back with her to Islamorada for moral support when she broke the news to David Gordon. Actually, looking back on it, Anne felt he likely wanted to see exactly what he had married; there is a little money, and then there is a lot of money. Leigh wanted to see whether he had married a little or a lot.

It had been quite a shock to him when the man discovered he wasn't going to get one red cent. David Gordon took one smell of Leigh and by some unknown method, correctly proclaimed his granddaughter's new husband a fortune hunter. Since the Gordons had never been known for keeping their mouths closed or their opinions to themselves, David Gordon made it very plain exactly how he felt.

Anne finished in the worst position imaginable, caught right in the middle, and made the worst possible mistake. She sided with Leigh against her grandfather, thus making any reconciliation unlikely.

After their leaving Islamorada amid massive recriminations on both sides, Anne and Leigh went back to New York. Since her new husband had ditched his security job with better prospects in view, the two of them now had no income; David Gordon had made it clear that not a dime more was forthcoming from him. Anne's mother helped, but her wedding gift of cash soon disappeared. So the newlyweds drifted from New York to California, where Leigh said "the action could be found."

The marriage hadn't been flourishing; however, Anne still felt besotted with her new husband. She got a job as a secretary in a law firm to pay the bills while Leigh made the rounds of the casting offices, always convinced that his big break had to be arriving soon. He just needed the right producer and director "to really appreciate his talents."

They drifted along in this manner for a while until the day when Anne became ill and left work early. She walked into the apartment and found her husband – surprised him, in fact. He was not alone.

Anne packed a bag and took the car on the grounds that her money had paid for it. Besides, Leigh had the apartment and the furniture for consolation. Anne left L.A. and drove straight east, away from California and the misery of her failed marriage. She drove for five days, nonstop, until she reached the sunny state of Florida.

Memories of Edward's death haunted her, so returning to Islamorada and Key West had never been an option. Moreover, David Gordon's words of blame still rang loud in her ears. With the money Anne made by selling the Porsche (Leigh had expensive tastes when it came to cars, too), she went to school nights in Miami, studying art and photography. The first night of class, Cristel Slivka introduced herself; six months later, they started a business together in Cedar Key on the west coast of Florida.

The business turned into a success, the first overwhelming success Anne had since before her nightmarish marriage, so she found a good lawyer and initiated divorce proceedings. The divorce finished her relationship with Leigh; and her newly found business boomed. Anne was delighted to find that there were so many parents in the world who eagerly paid so well for photographs of their beloved offspring.

71

Cristel specialized in outdoor pictures – children on horseback, swimming underwater and roller skating on the beaches of Cedar Key, while Anne did birthday parties and graduations.

Perhaps the best part of the new partnership was that the two got along famously, almost like sisters who had known each other for years; both loved art and creating original jewelry became a profitable sideline. Cristel seemed calm, easy-going and just what Anne needed. They had been talking about opening a branch in St. Augustine when the letter from Ben Caldwell arrived, bringing Anne back to Key West and Islamorada.

Her "psychology" seemed to be failing; sleep remained farther away than ever. The hall clock chimed one when Anne climbed out of bed with a weary sigh and stepped over to the window. The night wind felt still; in the distance lacy, milk-white foam spilled up onto the beach. The air below smelled sickly sweet from the hydrangeas and rhododendrons, a cloying, heavy scent. Anne left Jezebella curled up on the bed as she wandered out on the balcony to stare at the garden in the direction of the woods; then her eyes widened, and she choked, but couldn't turn away from the opposite side of the tree line.

The light appeared there, just as Diana Moon had claimed. A thin, little ray, that blinked on and off as someone moved through the palms; at last it held steady before moving upward toward the tree house.

Anne stood transfixed. Suddenly, she decided, turning and running toward the woods. Not more than thirty seconds later, she had bolted out of Gordon Hall, across the front porch and into the garden.

Chapter Eight

"About, about, in reel and rout
The death-fires danced at night;"
The Rime of the Ancient Mariner (Coleridge)

The flowers stretched all around, their sickly odor more penetrating up close. Anne moved down the garden walk, pushed through the shrubbery, and entered the woods.

She stopped, peering into the brush and trying to see the light. Not a glimmer pierced the blackness. She advanced into heavy shrubbery, the mosquitoes biting unmercifully in the undergrowth.

Then Anne heard a rustling that sounded like a raccoon or some other small, relatively harmless creature. She glanced nervously around; suddenly, it was there again, the feeling that someone watched her.

Twirling around, her eyes searched the greenery. Nothing could be seen. Yet, the feeling didn't depart; instead, it continued to grow stronger.

Her mouth felt dry as the breath rasped in her throat. Then the tree house came into sight, illuminated by a sliver of moonlight that somehow, managed to curl its way around the palms.

The tree house looked grotesque in the partial light, somewhat like a giant, malignant growth suspended in the air. Hesitating, Anne grasped the ladder and started to climb.

Halfway to the top, something reached out and twined around her. Twisting frantically, she finally realized it was just a rough piece of wood that had caught on her terry-cloth robe. With a final gasp, Anne dragged herself up onto the platform. From this height, it became possible to see a short way into the distance. Glancing down, she noted it was a long, long drop to the ground. She listened but the forest seemed quiet. Too quiet, with all sound extinguished.

The feeling remained, of eyes peering straight at her. Anne pushed the door open and walked inside the tree house. A faint glow illuminated the furniture. She ran her hand across the table until she found and lit the candle that lay there. The place seemed deserted, but the candle looked new; no wax had dripped down its side. Anne wandered past the chairs and over to the cupboard, yanked open the door and ducked instinctively. The only things inside were cans of food and a few plastic dishes with no dust on any of it.

A sudden soft sound caught her attention. As Anne strained to listen, she heard footsteps. Someone was moving directly below her position, his feet making a rustling noise while tramping through the underbrush. She smothered the candle and waited, every sense concentrated on the noise. The footsteps traced the sound of his movement away from the tree house.

Anne edged toward the ladder and peered downward; the woods seemed silent at that particular moment. Gathering her robe, she turned and crawled back down the ladder to the ground. Hesitating, she decided to follow the rustling in the underbrush, moving cautiously ahead as noiselessly as possible.

He moved away from the tree house and toward the water. Anne tried to remain calm while she considered what to do if he stopped. Suddenly, all became still and silence reigned.

She waited. No sound reached her straining ears. In the distance, the sea roared up onto the beach, making a hissing noise as it crossed the sand. Anne wasn't interested in the water; she wanted to find out which way the prowler had gone. Then she heard a clank of metal and abandoned caution to charge ahead.

Anne felt a swish of air as something hard and immovable crashed down on the back of her head. Agonizing pain followed by pinpricks of light seemed to blow apart under her eyelids. Her arms flayed around, trying to catch hold of anything within reach, as her body crashed to the sand. Staring up, she felt rather than saw a figure out of the corner of her eye. Tall and handsome; half-dazed, she squinted up at him, uncomprehending, before unconsciousness claimed her.

>>>>*Gordon*<<<<

A slit eyed moon glowed down on him as Alex Stryker drove rapidly toward Islamorada; it was late and he still needed to return to the boathouse, get the whaler and go back out to the *Riga*. His eyes narrowed in thought, his mind elsewhere. When he saw her body half-covered by sand, it took an extra second for him to react.

"Anne!" His foot hit the break on the jeep; the vehicle had barely stopped before he yanked open the door and ran to her side.

Anne lay sprawled in the sand, face down. Stryker could feel a pulse of fear begin to pound in his throat as he carefully turned her over. The gash on her forehead, dried with black blood, looked nasty, but he needed to get her inside where he could take care of her. Off of the beach, for sure! Stryker carefully scooped her up into his arms and moved toward the wharf and the boathouse. He shoved open the door and tenderly placed her on a worn navy blanket before flicking on the light. Then Stryker took a handkerchief and began to clean the clotted blood from her wound, his dark eyes anxiously watching her face.

If she's been seriously injured... Alex Stryker's hands clenched in fury. So much for his masquerade as a diver in Devlin's crew! He vowed to personally hunt down the party responsible and...

Suddenly, Anne opened her eyes, moaned and sat up. She peered at him, a dazed expression on her face. Then her eyes seemed to focus.

"I should have known it would be you. We meet again and in such charming surroundings."

He relaxed and began to breathe easier.

"You can't be badly hurt. You sound too much like your normal, pleasant self."

"How did you happen to be here? Or shouldn't I ask?"

He moved, pushing himself away from the barrel on which he'd been leaning.

"I found you on the beach, unconscious, so I brought you in here. Now it's my turn. Do you have any idea what happened?"

Anne sank back on her temporary bed of navy blanket and life preservers and closed her eyes.

"There was a light in the tree house where Edward and I used to play when we were children. Diana Moon told me about it and she was right. Anyway, I came out and followed someone. I never did see who it was. Only I guess I got too close and he clobbered me."

Stryker frowned. His brows drew together as he studied her thoughtfully with a sphinx-eyed look.

Anne shivered and then struggled to rise.

"I wouldn't try to get up just yet. Besides, I have more questions to ask you."

She choked.

"You have some questions? What about me? How did you come to be here, and what did you see – the prowler in the tree house, or someone else?"

"Look, there's nothing sinister about it. I was on my way back from Key West in the jeep. I got down near the wharf and saw you lying there. I brought you in here, since it was the closest place. End of story."

Anne shrugged. "Did you see anyone on the beach? Besides me, that is?"

"Uh-uh. You were all by your lonesome." He paused. "Did you recognize the person you were trying to follow? Even an impression might help."

"No!" A very definite negative, that caused Stryker to glance up sharply. "He was just a figure moving away through the trees. I'm not sure if it was a man or a woman."

"You might have something there. If Diana Moon told you about that light, she might have been trying to set you up."

Anne's brows furrowed.

"She doesn't strike me as being the type to be lurking around in the undergrowth."

Stryker continued. "Don't be fooled by her appearance. Some of the most harmless looking people turn out to be quite dangerous. You read about them in the newspaper all the time."

"Are you speaking from experience?" Anne muttered sarcastically, easing herself to a sitting position.

He ignored the outburst.

"Seriously, you seem to be slightly accident prone. I'd stay away from people I haven't known for most of my life if I were you. After all, the murderer could be anyone!"

"Including you?" She seemed to want to shake him somehow.

Stryker stayed calm and didn't rise to her bait.

"Yes," he said softly. "Even me."

Her head jerked erect at this. Stryker stared at her steadily with his mesmerizing eyes, rather like a cobra watching its prey. She rose suddenly.

"Look, I'd better be getting back. It's late and I'll have enough trouble getting in as it is. I'm going to have a full day tomorrow. There's something I have to take care of for Diana Moon."

"What's Miss Moon's problem this time?" He followed, as they moved outside and toward Gordon Hall.

"I promised that an old friend of mine would come and look at the situation on the *Riga*. See if he can find out who, or what, may be causing all the trouble. He's a boatman named Saunders –Tom Saunders, and he knows every legend, every cove at Islamorada. His brother works at the Hemingway House and I'm hoping to talk to him and get a lead on Tom's location."

"I wish you luck. Take care of yourself, Anne." He hesitated, wanting to say so much more, but she'd already moved away. His eyes followed her as she walked inland, pushing through the rhododendron bushes to the lawn.

He saw Anne pause and glance back only once. Stryker raised his hand in a brief wave before turning away and moving back toward the boathouse. Tomorrow. Anne would be talking to Saunders' brother tomorrow. Stryker's brows knit in worry. He couldn't stop her from seeing the fellow, but he could call Armando Catalano at the police station in Key West and apprise him of the situation. The local police could keep an eye on everything – just in case her visit with Saunders turned out to be more than either of them had bargained for.

Chapter Nine

"One more Unfortunate, Weary of breath,"
The Bridge of Sighs – (Thomas Hood)

Quietly, Anne eased inside, through the back door by the kitchen. A black shape slid outside and disappeared into the undergrowth – Jezebella, going for a nightly prowl. Aside from the black cat, the house felt still as Anne crossed the hall and reached the staircase. Suddenly, she heard voices speaking in a murmur; it sounded as though they had stopped on the veranda.

Perhaps the events of the past twenty-four hours combined with Alex Stryker's warning had made an impression. Two people had died, likely murdered, and Anne never hesitated. She slipped forward through the main room over to the heavily-curtained window, and peered out from behind her grandfather's expensive draperies, trying to be inconspicuous. The two people were locked in a tight embrace completely oblivious to their surroundings; they would not have noticed a palm tree falling on the house.

The moon had been covered by the clouds but now it appeared, drenching them in a white, almost artificial light. The man and woman stood illuminated for a few seconds before clouds obscured the moon once more, leaving the veranda dappled in gray light. But not before Anne had recognized the ruthlessly attractive features of Jack Cole and seen the long, dark-brown hair of the girl looking soulfully into his eyes, waiting expectantly for his kiss.

Anne crept away, feeling like some kind of voyeur. Her one thought as she tip-toed up the main stairs and slithered down the hall to her room concerned how to deal with her younger cousin, Robin.

>>>>*Gordon*<<<<

Despite the late hours, Anne awoke early the following morning. The blazing sun sizzled outside as she dressed as cool as possible for comfort in shorts and a blouse before opening her door. Roger Devlin, captain of the *San Pedro* salvage operation, walked out of David Gordon's room with Maud following close behind. The frozen smile on her face plainly indicated that she didn't like having her brother disturbed at this hour of the day for sunken treasure or anything else.

In sharp contrast to their previous meeting, Devlin seemed in a pleasant mood – and far more approachable.

People usually do feel more pleasant, Anne reflected to herself, *when not making murder accusations and finding dead bodies.* She ruminated on the events that had occurred over the past weeks. Two divers, both dead, accidents galore, curses on the entire ship salvage project, plus astrology theories and a movie company cluttering up the scene – a veritable hodge-podge of events. Anne felt her head spinning at the enormity of what Devlin had had to contend with in a very brief time. She shook her head to try and clear it then concentrated on the person standing before her.

Her attention focused on a large, jagged scar running half-way down the man's left arm; it looked like

81

the bite of a fish. As she craned her neck, he answered her unspoken question.

"It was an eel, Miss Gordon." Today his voice sounded soft and cultured; he might have been a marine biology professor setting off to meet a college class.

As Devlin crossed the hall, Maud banged the door shut to her brother's room. The woman didn't like Devlin, and he confirmed this in his next statement to Anne.

"Your aunt doesn't care much for visitors, especially me," he added succinctly. "Says I get the old gentleman too excited by half. But excitement is good for a person. It gives him something to look forward to, something to stay alive for. It would be worth the money David Gordon's spent, even if we didn't find a thing!"

He fell into step as they walked down the heavily-carpeted stairs. Anne looked over at him curiously.

"Is that why you do it, Mr. Devlin? I heard talk of some gold coins and a necklace. But it's not what you find, but how you feel about it then?"

"In part. My father was a dirt-poor farmer in Ohio. I tried it for a while, but there sure wasn't any excitement in that. Got into diving accidently when I came down here one winter. Didn't want to leave and I needed an excuse to stay around, so I signed on at a dive shop, selling scuba equipment. There wasn't any excitement in staying on land, watching every dolt who thought he knew how to dive go out. So I went into the treasure business. And I was lucky, really lucky. Had a strike and I got a lot of good publicity. I haven't been out of customers since, and it's been over thirty years."

"But what have you actually found out there, Mr. Devlin?" They reached the bottom of the stairs and she turned to face him.

"Pure gold, Miss Gordon. Found in the mines by the Indians and on its way to Spain. But why don't you come out and see for yourself? You can watch the entire operation plus see what we've found. I'll even throw in a grand tour of the *Riga*. She's a great little ship that I made over to my personal specifications. Originally she was a minesweeper in the War." He stopped his enthusiastic account to take a breath.

"I'd love to come – as soon as possible."

The man beamed. If he had anything to hide on the *Riga* about the murders or anything else, it certainly didn't show.

"Good! I heard you've done some diving. Maybe you could get some pictures of the ship and the *San Pedro* dive sight while you're visiting. Publicity is so important, you know," he finished up ingeniously.

Roger Devlin smiled, an innocent, half-hopeful, half-whimsical smile that turned up the corners of his mouth and made him seem like a small boy asking for an ice-cream cone. Anne found herself giving in to his infectious grin in spite of herself.

"All right. I'll take pictures for you. I can easily see why you never had trouble getting backers for any of your ventures. Only no diving. I'm a little out of condition."

He took the statement at face value. "Okay. I'll send Stryker in with the whaler. Say about one o'clock tomorrow?" He turned and with a cheerful wave, exited through the front door.

Anne wandered slowly back to the dining room; it was empty. Even Jezebella had abandoned Gordon Hall to prowl elsewhere. Anne poured coffee from the buffet and sat down. Although the movie company wouldn't be up until noon, she did wonder about Colin and Robin.

Today would be an ideal time to try and locate Tom Saunders by questioning his brother, Gary. With all the odd things that had been happening, maybe Gary Saunders could give some clue as to where their boatman had found employment; possibly she could persuade him to come back to Islamorada by one means or another. Having reached a decision, Anne finished the coffee, went out to her car, and started on the short trip into town.

The sun beamed down, creating a beautiful day as Anne cruised along. The sea seemed like clear, translucent glass, the kind of water where one could see down into the depths for ninety or one hundred feet with no effort at all. Gulls and brown pelicans soared overhead as Anne turned east on U.S. 1 and followed the route into the center of Key West, where she drove down the narrow streets, which were canopied by Bengal-rose colored Poinciana trees.

Around her, people worked despite the hot day; the air reeked with a curious mixture of odors amid the bustle of activity. The houses here seemed small, clapboard types, very New Englandish, with their widows-walks circling the tops. Decades ago, sea captains of the Keys had watched for ships going aground off the reefs, waiting for the bounty that would be theirs to salvage, should they reach the vessel first.

>>>>*Gordon*<<<<

Anne parked the car in front of the Lighthouse Museum with its World War II Japanese submarine out

84

on the front lawn. The light could no longer be lit, but the tower could be seen from all prominent parts of the Key.

She walked across the street to the shade-covered Hemingway home. Here the noted writer had created some of his most well-known literary works like *For Whom the Bell Tolls.* No tour buses stood in front of the house yet, but Anne knew they would be along later in the day. After paying the admission to the ticket-seller, the girl learned that Saunders' brother, Gary, had been assigned as guide for the first group out. Hopefully, there would be a chance for her to talk with him at the end of the tour.

For the next hour and a half, she learned about Ernest Hemingway, who had lived in this home until his death in 1961. Gary Saunders, a virtual walking library, had an inexhaustible store of information concerning not just Hemingway, but also his family.

The colonial white house had green trim and remained cool and inviting inside, despite the heat. The group meandered from the living room to the dining room with its stuffed animal heads above the door, souvenirs of Hemingway's adventures in Africa, the setting for several of his novels. A long, shining glass fish perched on the table serving as a centerpiece, another example of the author's love of outdoor sports. The next door kitchen had been frequented by Hemingway, who enjoyed cooking; the counter had been raised to accommodate his height.

Anne had a chance to study Gary Saunders as they went upstairs; Tom's brother seemed tall and thin with glasses that kept sliding down his nose. He moved quickly and gesticulated constantly with his hands, pointing out the draperies in the master bedroom, the fireplace in the governess' room, the memorabilia in what had once been the boys' room. One of Hemingway's wives had been a decorator and it showed; good taste predominated throughout the mansion. Across from the upstairs porch, a family of curious raccoons in a nearby tree eyed the morning crop of visitors.

The group progressed to the back of the house to see the swimming pool and the cottage where Hemingway had actually done his writing. Anne noticed several of the tourists surreptitiously touching the inside walls, which they could reach from the doorway, as though hoping that the great man's genius would rub off on them. Descendants of Hemingway's cats clustered here, there and everywhere, many with the famous six toes. They had been loved by the writer; he named them after all of his friends and the custom had been continued. Anne picked up "Zelda Fitzgerald" and tickled her under the chin, when Gary Saunders announced the tour's end. While the rest of the group rushed to the vending machines for needed refreshment, she saw a chance to talk to the guide.

Detaching herself from "Zelda", Anne moved toward Gary, who peered at a little girl fondling one of the kittens. He seemed to be expecting a comment about the tour. At least she surprised him in that.

"You don't know me, Mr. Saunders, but my name is Gordon. Anne Gordon – from Islamorada."

Gary put down the soft drink he held; a look of caution and suspicion crossed his face.

"Ah yes, Islamorada. I remember Tom talking about you, Miss Gordon. I heard there has been a lot of excitement there lately. Something about a Spanish ship being found off the reef – pieces of eight and all."

Anne's eyes widened in shock. Gary Saunders had not even mentioned the trouble at Islamorada. His eyes

86

focused on one of the kittens crawling by his shoe. How had her grandfather managed to conceal the two deaths? By hook or crook, more likely the latter. Colin had undoubtedly done the dirty work, but David Gordon would have planned it.

"Yes, it's true. I'm going to see the wreck tomorrow. I'll be taking photos for publicity."

"That's what you went into then? After you left Islamorada?"

"Uh-huh. But I'm home, at least for the time being. My grandfather hasn't been well, and I wanted to be close. Although that isn't what I wanted to ask you about."

His eyes looked a question before he turned around slowly, taking note of the tall trees and the turquoise-colored sky above.

"It must have taken a lot for him to leave all this. Hemingway, I mean. It's about as close to heaven as you'll ever get on earth." The man's sadness was apparent.

Anne shifted uneasily. Death and sadness seemed to be twins everywhere.

"He was a marvelous novelist – such a shame to die by suicide. He had so much talent. But…it was cut short."

"Yes. But we all have to go, one way or another." Gary Saunders stated unnecessarily.

Anne glanced at him sharply. Had the man in fact referred to more than just Hemingway's death? Had he in an oblique way just warned her of something?

"What was it you wanted to know?" The mood shattered, like the undercurrent of the sea had erased it.

"I'm interested in talking to your brother, Tom, about Islamorada. He worked there for such a long time and knew so much about the shoreline. There have been some small diving incidents and Mr. Grant suggested your brother might have information that could help." She stopped. Better not to say too much, at least not right away.

Several long moments passed. Children ran down the steps below them; overhead, a brown pelican soared, wings silhouetted fan-shaped against the light of the sun.

Gary Saunders drew himself up.

"Mr. Grant is right. Tom did know a lot about the coastline down that way. He should have. He worked for your grandfather long enough." Gary shifted position. "But those weren't diving incidents, Miss Gordon. You know it as well as I."

"What do you mean?"

"All Key West knows. When one diver gets caught and minced into bits and the other has a malfunction of equipment, it's pretty certain, unless Devlin has been hiring blasted amateurs. With David Gordon's money, that's hardly likely."

So much for a subtle approach! He had known from the beginning what she'd wanted! "All right, Mr. Saunders. I'll level with you. I should have in the first place and saved some time. There's been trouble, which is why I wanted to talk to Tom. See if I couldn't coax him back to Islamorada. Is he still in Key West, or elsewhere?"

"So it's like that, is it? The whims of the rich! You wave your hand and expect Tom to just come right along, like a kitten getting reeled in by a piece of string?"

88

Suddenly Gary Saunders' tone changed. The obvious resentment flared up and then died from his eyes.

"Sorry. He's been up in Orlando the last week or so – at one of the amusement parks. Got a good job working a ride there."

After a little coaxing, Gary fumbled through his pockets and found a card with Tom's contact information written on it. He reluctantly handed the card to Anne.

"Thank you. I'll go and see him. Maybe he can help me straighten this tangle out." Anne held out a hand. Gary Saunders ignored it and went on, almost as though she hadn't spoken.

"He got out on purpose, Miss Gordon – got out and away from Islamorada. You'd do well to follow! No good will come of bringing that gold up from the sea. The curse, it's gotten two of the divers. And it will get more! Mark my words!"

The man's face dripped with sweat; his eyes had a strange, glassy appearance and seemed to flare with an inner light.

Anne opened her mouth to tell Gary Saunders not to believe in superstitious nonsense, but she couldn't choke out the words. And when the man pulled away from her as though she had leprosy, Anne let him scurry off and didn't attempt to follow.

Chapter Ten

"There is no vice so simple,
but assumes some mark of virtue"
– The Merchant of Venice (Shakespeare)

Anne didn't remember leaving the Hemingway House and getting into the Volkswagen. Gary Saunders' words kept playing over and over, like a tape recorder that stuck and wouldn't shut off. Tom worked in Orlando. The next move in this shadow-dance would be to catch a plane and go to see the man. If Mohammed wouldn't come to the mountain, the mountain would have to go to him. It seemed to be the only solution for finding out what she wanted to know.

The short flight to Orlando from the Key West International Airport was completely uneventful. Gary Saunders had given Anne his brother's telephone number; she called him on her cell 'phone from the car rental station in Orlando. It seemed Tom Saunders worked in Water World, operating, ironically enough, a submarine ride based on Jules Verne's, *Twenty Thousand Leagues under the Sea*. Anne needed to contact him there, to listen and to talk and hopefully he'd provide some answers to the puzzle at Islamorada.

Anne followed the Interstate into the huge Lake Buena Vista area and parked the rental car in the Water World lot. The place had filled up early; although it had turned warm, people crowded into the park, ignoring the heat. The sky remained a deep cerulean blue in a gorgeous day. Anne found herself wishing that she had come to enjoy this place like all of the other hundreds of visitors. Perhaps sometime it might be possible to return with nothing more on her mind than whether to go swimming or use the water slide, when all of the problems at Islamorada had been resolved.

Anne rode the guest train into the transportation and ticket center, where she collected a ticket, map and brochure for Water World. Aside from the rides, many people thronged toward the outdoor pavilion where a show featuring "Little Hatchet," a baby whale, had just started.

Consulting the map, it appeared the submarine ride, where Tom Saunders worked, could be found at the far edge of the park. Anne had a choice to go either by ferry boat or monorail to reach the entranceway to the main attractions. The monorail left in five minutes, which made the choice simple.

The train filled rapidly. As it swayed gently out into space, she looked over the lush, green vegetation below. The park had been built on what had once been a swamp, loaded with rattlesnakes and oversized mosquitoes; now the swamp water had been channeled into a beautiful lake that glistened as the afternoon sun filtered down. The monorail crossed over shrubbery that had been cleverly trimmed into the shapes of water animals, first zooming past a dolphin, then a whale and a sea horse peering out of the greenery. Staring hard, Anne could almost imagine that they swam across the bluish-green grass, which swept by below; the wind, blowing southeast across the lake, made the grasses tremble as though the animals had come to life.

The train jerked to a halt at the entrance to the park; she disembarked along with the other passengers, trying to attach herself inconspicuously to a small group as though belonging. Yet suddenly, Anne felt herself break out into a cold sweat; the gut-wrenching fear returned that someone in this happy, chattering crowd watched her.

She scanned the closest people, but nobody stepped back, guiltily or otherwise. As a matter of fact, nobody seemed to be paying the slightest bit of attention to anything besides having a good time.

Anne muttered under her breath about having an overactive imagination. This whole trip had been on the spur of the moment; nobody knew she had planned to come, so how could anyone have followed? In spite of these logical thoughts, she hurried down Center Street with its water slide and flying fish ride. Eventually Anne looked up and saw the *Twenty Thousand Leagues Under the Sea* submarine ride.

She stopped at an available bench, sat down, and studied the crowd coming from behind. It looked like the people couldn't have cared less about much of anything; adults and children seemed to be shouting, eating, or arguing about which ride to go on next. Shrugging, Anne got in line and ended up on a seat in the sub. The ride ran on a track under a large-sized lake; while the passengers stared through plate-glass windows, everything from fake fish that wriggled realistically to a blue-eyed mermaid, who winked a long-lashed eye, passed in front of them. The true-to-life figures seemed so real, Anne almost believed in some of the enchantment.

She looked around the inside of the "vessel." All the tourists oohed and aahed at what flashed past outside, almost as though on cue. Then Anne felt, rather than saw, someone standing close.

"It's all right, Miss Gordon." Tom Saunders spoke in a low drawl. "I just wanted to make sure you'd come alone."

Anne turned. Brown eyes stared into green.

"I'm just interested in finding out about my twin brother's death five years ago."

"Are you sure he died?" Tom Saunders hissed back at her.

Anne's face whitened; her throat went dry.

"What do you mean?"

"They never did recover his body from that cave, now did they?"

"No, I…no, they didn't."

"I always liked you, Miss Gordon. And maybe I can tell you a few things you'd care to know."

Anne leaned back weakly against a wall. She faintly heard the voice of the late actor, James Mason, doing a commentary about the wonders of the deep.

Tom Saunders glanced around nervously.

"Look, this isn't a good place to talk. We'll have to go elsewhere!"

"You're telling me! Do you have a break this afternoon? I could meet you somewhere."

Saunders hesitated. "I don't get off again until four o'clock."

He frowned.

"All right. By the Shark Attack Pool. But leave for now. Besides, the ride is almost over."

Amid the delighted shrieks of the children, Mr. Mason wound up his spiel.

"Okay. By the Shark Attack Pool." Anne licked dry lips. "It's very important to me, Mr. Saunders, and it could matter to you, too!"

Saunders' face reflected annoyance.

"I said I'd meet you there and I will." He turned and made his way back to the *bridge* of the vessel.

She disembarked with the rest of the passengers and checked the time. There was almost an hour to kill, so Anne decided to wander around the park, see the sights, and maybe have something to eat.

Suddenly, miraculously, the strange feeling of being watched vanished. Anne felt relieved. Her nerves had had an especially overactive time; a logical explanation could be found for almost anything.

She strolled to the main square, past a steamboat ride and a desert island. The time went fast; it was suddenly five to four when Anne approached the Shark Attack Pool. Children and adults lined up to crawl out onto the floating discs; the discs ran on an underwater track where "sharks" attacked beneath the water. Children shrieked with excitement while parents mopped at wet clothes and faces. The fake plastic sharks went round and round the discs, coming in closer and closer for the kill.

Anne became aware that four o'clock had passed and no Saunders had put in an appearance. She trudged back and forth in front of the Shark Attack ride, her eyes scanning the entire Water World area. Perhaps he'd gotten held up or maybe he had never meant to come at all, but had only promised, just to get away. Somehow, Anne couldn't believe it. The old Tom Saunders would have shown up. As the minutes ticked by, her uneasiness increased; it looked as though she would just have to go and see if he couldn't be located.

94

Anne gave it another half-hour, just to be sure. More likely, the feeling of foreboding which swelled inside her had kept her glued to the area around the Shark Attack ride. Four-thirty approached as she wandered toward the nearest ticket booth. Finally the seller looked up; Anne approached and asked about the missing Saunders.

The ticket saleswoman sized her up and down. She must have decided that this young woman was a relative or friend, because she finally answered the question. Or perhaps it was the look of desperation that Anne could no longer hide.

"The employees' lockers are under the aquarium across from the Flying Fish ride – right off the Center Square. He might have gone down there."

Anne mumbled a thank you and darted off. Making her way past the Happy Trout Restaurant and the Dolphin Arcade, she almost ran toward the Flying Fish ride. The crowd had partially evaporated because of the dinner hour and the place was relatively empty.

Anne peered around. Across the way appeared a triangular-shaped building, painted dark blue with white, wave-like trim. "Fish Haven" told Anne she had come to the right place. She yanked open the door to the aquarium and stepped inside; cool dark air flooded over her. Fish in their tanks swam slowly back and forth, fins waving, eyes staring hypnotically through the glass.

A sign to the employees' locker room pointed down some stairs. Two people stood at a nearby vending machine in the aquarium aisle; as a man, woman, and four children stopped to join them, Anne moved casually over, turned the door handle, walked inside and down the steps.

An escalator ran to the basement level. Anne rode down, casting frantic looks around, hoping that nobody would stop and start asking questions. Fortunately, the place appeared empty of anyone to ask anything, including Tom Saunders. Anne reached the lowest level and looked nervously here and there, but the area seemed deserted.

She ran down one aisle of lockers and back up another. The longish, nondescript room seemed exactly the same as a million other locker rooms all over the world. Walls, ceiling, and floor had been painted the typical battleship gray, while harsh, artificial light glared down from overhead, bare bulbs. Anne saw the inevitable bulletin board in the far corner covered with all kinds of notices, next to a drinking fountain. But no Tom Saunders.

Anne stopped, breathing hard. Then she felt it. Someone else stood in the room. Her eyes searched frantically, as a cold stillness enveloped the locker room, reminding her of a morgue. She began retracing her steps toward the escalator, her feet echoing hollowly.

Anne peered into every nook and cranny, but the place was empty. Tom Saunders had bolted the traces, so to speak, and vanished. But did he really disappear, Anne wondered to herself. Maybe I should call the police, but…

Suppose the man had just had second thoughts and stood her up? It could be as simple as that. Or maybe he had decided to try and sell his information to someone who would offer more? Or perhaps…they hadn't offered anything at all but his life?

Anne shook her head. She couldn't tell, but suddenly she wanted to get out of the tomb-like locker room. And when two gum-chewing, uniform clad female employees appeared and started down the escalator steps, Anne decided she'd had enough of the underground hole. She scrambled rapidly back upstairs and bolted out into the dappled sunlight.

Chapter Eleven

"What d'ye leave to your sister,
Lord Randal, my son?
What d'ye leave to your sister,
My handsome young man?"
"My gold and my silver, mak my bed soon
For I'm sick at the heart, an I fain wad lie down."
Lord Randal (Anonymous)

"Dead? You did say dead?" Alex Stryker thought he had misunderstood Officer Armando Catalano when the younger man had called him in the late afternoon.

"Yeah. The Orlando Police just telephoned. A Tom Sanders was discovered in his apartment lying in his shower with the water running. It seemed that the tenant downstairs had water leaking through the ceiling and called the landlord to complain."

Stryker rubbed the area over his eyes. It felt like he was developing the mother of all migraine headaches.

Catalano paused. "That's not all."

"Oh?" The silence held for several seconds.

"No. It seems Anne Gordon was the last person to see Saunders alive. Someone remembered her talking to the man when he was supposed to be working, running a submarine ride at Water World. They reported him – seems this guy felt that Saunders wasn't doing his job properly, of all things."

98

"But why did Anne go to Orlando? She was supposed to talk to Gary Saunders, the brother, at the Hemingway House."

"We had someone tailing her, just for protection. Ms. Gordon must have picked up the lead after talking to Gary Saunders. My officer trailed her when she left, but got stuck in traffic and lost her. He had no idea she would take a plane and go to Orlando. But…"

"I know. It couldn't look more suspicious!"

There was another even longer silence as Stryker's mind turned cartwheels and processed this new information. He couldn't believe that Anne had had anything to do with the murder. *Murders*, he corrected himself silently. Because the events on the *Riga* had been murder. He felt convinced of it. Stryker couldn't ignore his feelings for Anne, regardless of the fact that it might be clouding his judgment. Seriously so!

"What are you going to do?" Catalano finally queried.

Stryker smiled grimly.

"Roger Devlin told me earlier that he'd planned to go to dinner at Islamorada tonight. Discuss the salvage project with that finance guy, Colin Grant. And see how much longer those movie people are going to be prowling all over the dive ship. I'll get myself invited and go with him."

"You think somebody might give something away?"

"Who knows? I think there's a good possibility that somebody in that room killed at least one person. Perhaps we'll get lucky and find out who it is."

"My money is on Anne Gordon. I don't believe in coincidence and her turning up in Orlando right before Tom Saunders died…" Catalano's voice trailed off.

Stryker didn't believe in coincidence either, which presented him with a gigantic problem.

"Keep me posted," he said cryptically to Catalano before he switched off his cell 'phone.

>>>>Gordon<<<<

The short, direct flight back to Key West left late from the Orlando Airport. A different plane had to be substituted at the last minute due to "mechanical problems." Anne moved in a daze, following the rest of the passengers, from one line through security and back into another line. She instinctively felt that Tom Saunders had known essential information, probably the truth of what had happened at Islamorada – but what truth?

Incredible though it seemed, she arrived at Gordon Hall just in time for dinner. David Gordon was too ill to come down and Maud had elected to stay upstairs to keep him company, but the movie people were there, along with Robin. Colin arrived very late, but did finally put in an appearance. But Anne's attention focused on Alex Stryker, who had arrived promptly at eight o'clock with Roger Devlin. She watched him detach himself from Devlin and slide through the crowd toward her.

Anne could feel the flush stain her cheeks as she confronted Stryker. She hadn't seen him in such formal attire before, but the dark suit and tie he wore just seemed to accentuate his rugged good looks.

"Anne."

Even her name on his lips seemed to excite her. The everyday somehow sounded special, unique, although

100

maybe that stemmed from the fact that the man saying it was so unique in himself. Diana Moon certainly seemed to think so as she abandoned Frank Blaine and elbowed her way over to Stryker's side.

Ignoring Anne, she turned to the diver.

"I saw you come in," she gushed, limpid eyed, "and I just had to come over and say hello."

As the woman prattled on, Anne caught Stryker's eye as he grinned slightly. Diana reminded her of a shark latching onto its prey; once the jaws had closed, there was just no escaping.

The gong for dinner rang at that moment as Stryker purposely trailed the two women toward the dining room. Unfortunately, Diana maneuvered herself into a place directly next to him with Frank Blaine on the other side. Anne sat much farther down, close to her cousin Robin and Aldridge Thornton. Listening to Diana warble on nonstop, rather like a demented parrot, Anne reflected grimly that it was going to be very long dinner.

Anne watched Stryker and Diana Moon out of the corner of one eye; it seemed the actress was more than slightly attracted to the rugged diver. Her own attention was eventually claimed by the scriptwriter, Aldridge Thornton, who kept everyone enthralled with interesting tidbits of information that he had learned in the library at Islamorada.

Anne looked around at all the normal people talking about normal things and tried to forget about how her day had been wasted. Meanwhile, Aldridge babbled happily on.

"It's incredible. The *San Pedro* was loaded with treasure, over six hundred gold bars and nine hundred silver ones. And all the passengers would have had jewelry on them when the ship went down."

Robin glanced up curiously.

"But how did they know exactly what was supposed to be on the galleon, Mr. Thornton?"

"By the manifest list. The King's agents were here, there, and everywhere, rather like the Scarlet Pimpernel in France two hundred years later. The agents recorded amounts of money most accurately for the tax that had to be paid. As a matter-of-fact they seemed almost obsessed with getting every last item down, half-a-dozen times over."

Anne felt a prick of interest in what Thornton said.

"Didn't the Spaniards have any idea where the *San Pedro* went down? Couldn't they have tried to salvage it themselves?"

"They did, Ms. Gordon. Try that is. But they had very primitive diving equipment. No underwater breathing apparatus, naturally. That didn't come along until Jacques Cousteau. But they did have tortoise shells that were used for goggles. And the abilities of some of those slaves the Spaniards captured were amazing. They could hold their breath underwater for four, maybe five minutes!"

"But what happened to the *San Pedro* in the first place?" Robin persisted. "Is anyone sure?"

"We've had scholars checking in the archives of Seville. The *San Pedro* put into Havana where the treasure that had been shipped overland from the mines in Mexico was loaded on board." He lowered his voice surreptitiously. "That's how the legend about a curse started – because of the slaves – so many of them lost their lives through ill-treatment by the Spaniards. They are the ones who are supposed to have cursed it."

Anne took a sip of water.

"Did the *San Pedro* sink because of a storm?" she asked, hoping to get Aldridge away from the topic of the curse, which everyone seemed to be so fond of talking about.

Diana Moon, her blue eyes practically protruding out of her face, stared intently at Thornton from the other end of the table.

"A violent hurricane, Miss Gordon. The *San Pedro* was part of a fleet of eleven ships that left Havana in the spring of 1622, but the storm knocked the entire group so far off course, that three of the ships ran aground and sank. Spain was able to recover most of the treasure from the *Rossario* and the *Castalano*, but the *San Pedro* was the last in the line. She went down in water over twenty feet deep. And there was no way the gold could be brought to the surface from that depth. Not in those days."

Thornton stopped to nibble a bit of shrimp from the plate in front of him, but his enthusiasm refused to be diminished.

"Over the years the sand on the ocean floor covered a good deal of the wreck. But the *San Pedro* was split wide open like an overripe melon. She spilled her guts out for miles all along this coast!"

"I'm sure that's very interesting, Aldridge. And you've definitely done your homework, but must we spend the entire evening talking about it?" Frank Blaine's voice spoke out, harsh and somewhat guttural.

Anne stared at him in surprise. This rudeness seemed to be another aspect of the man's character that didn't show up on the movie screen.

Alex Stryker studied the actor intently but remained silent.

"We all find it interesting, darling," Diana Moon interjected. Her roving eyes wandered down the table and she smiled as if to make amends for Blaine's outburst. Strangely, Anne began to like the actress very much.

Thornton had stopped talking for a few brief moments, but now he started up again.

"You'll see, Frank – and you too, Mr. James. They're recovering more and more of the treasure every day, and it will make a great story."

His eyes took on a dreamy look. Watching the man, Anne believed he saw himself getting next year's Academy Award for the best screenplay.

"The Lost Treasure of the San Pedro," he mumbled. "Or how about 'The Secret of Barren Reef?'"

"What about 'Sink, Sank, Sunk,'" put in Peter James waspishly. "Give it a rest, Aldridge. Let's leave treasure trouble for tonight and talk about something else."

Diana Moon visibly brightened.

"Peter, did you know that tomorrow is supposed to be an especially lucky day for you? The position of the sun is aligned with Saturn in such a way…"

Anne laughed aloud.

Stryker grinned.

James' glared; he looked like he wanted to close his hands around Diana's neck and start squeezing. But he couldn't kill the goose that would be starring in his next film epic and smash that golden egg.

Meanwhile Aldridge Thornton fell silent; he busied himself making a design with his spoon in his very soft ice-cream. Now that attention had been diverted from him, the writer looked quite miserable to be completely cut from the limelight and out in the cold.

The party broke up shortly after.

Anne noticed Frank Blaine hovering in the corner with Peter James, gossiping about someone or something. Diana Moon looked disgusted with both of them and seemed to be spending her time talking to Aldridge Thornton. Devlin left, saying he had an early day on board the *Riga*. Anne watched Stryker, but he finally turned and followed Devlin when he saw Robin hovering close to her. The younger woman twisted a gold encrusted ring nervously around on her third finger as Anne looked a question at her.

"I know you're going to see my grandfather, and I...er...I mean Jack and I wondered if you'd put in a good word for us. Jack is such a marvelous person! Just look at this awesome friendship ring he gave me! Emeralds and opals! Things didn't go well at the luncheon the other day. And I thought maybe you would help!"

Anne remembered David Gordon's initial reaction to Jack Cole. That, plus the fact that Cole could be responsible for the murders, made her reluctant to speak well about him to anyone.

Robin caught her look.

"I know what you're thinking. But Jack is one of the good guys. I'm positive of it!"

"How?" Anne interrupted bluntly. Cole's toothpaste smile lingered in her mind.

"Why because of his eyes!"

"I beg your pardon?"

"His eyes!"

Anne still looked blank so Robin elaborated.

"In the comics, the bad guys always squint. The good guys have round eyes. Haven't you ever noticed? And Jack is a round eye," she finished up triumphantly.

Anne winced.

"You honestly expect me to give serious consideration to that prattle? Maybe your squinty eyed villains have allergies. Did you ever think about that? Going to Radcliffe," Anne observed dryly, "certainly has opened your mind!"

"I don't care what you say! It's a foolproof way to tell good from evil! And it's not any worse than Diana Moon's astrology!"

Anne turned away.

"I'll speak to our grandfather, if he's not asleep, about Jack Cole. But none of this eye business! I might end up being committed!"

Robin minced off, looking happier. The decisions of the young, Anne thought silently to herself. Then an unbidden picture appeared. Stryker's eyes had been round as could be, yet Tom and Gary Saunders both had a squint. Could it mean…

She shook her head in disgust and meandered up the winding staircase to her grandfather's room. Maud, dressed in a dowdy brown dress, stared coldly out after her first short rap on the door. She warmed up a bit when she saw Anne.

David Gordon lay on the bed, his face parchment-white, his breathing so slow that he seemed to be scarcely alive at all. Anne slipped into a chair and put her fingers over his.

Poor thing, she thought. His skin feels so dry. It could almost wither and dissolve in my hand.

"He's been sleeping for the last couple of hours," Maud said unnecessarily.

"Will he wake before morning?"

"I doubt it. There was a time when David would wake instantly if someone came into the room, but not any longer."

Anne turned to peer back at his face, feeling the tears beginning to form under her eyelids.

"The treasure business is what has kept him going the past couple of months. He's not a religious man, but it seemed as though the thought of making money while lying here in a bed was a comfort to him. Now they've had all of this trouble, and nobody is even sure if there are large portions of the treasure still to be recovered. He's slowly losing interest."

Anne placed his hand back under the blankets and rose to leave. As she turned, her attention focused on a figure moving cautiously across the back lawn. Maud stiffened, indicating that she had seen Robin, too.

"Perhaps it will just blow over."

Maud looked grim.

"Not a chance. He's another one," she muttered under her breath. "Another…"

"Like Leigh? I promise I'll do what I can to break it up. If that's possible."

Maud nodded silently. She stood straight and still, like a sentinel of death beside her brother's bed.

Chapter Twelve

"Mad, bad, and dangerous to know."
Journal (Lady Caroline Lamb)

It took Anne a long time to fall asleep that night. She sat on the veranda with Jezebella curled up at her feet and thought about Tom Saunders standing her up and the two divers, dead from the sea. In Agatha Christie murder mysteries, there was always a pattern of sorts to the crime. Anne tried to take each event that had happened and fit it into some sort of pattern; the problem stemmed from the fact that she just didn't seem to have enough information to determine anything. Each person at Islamorada seemed to be two people, what they appeared to be opposed to what they actually were. Eventually her mind just shut off as she eased into bed and fell into a sound sleep.

The dark shape loomed above, reaching out as Anne twisted and attempted to scream. Two deaths, two people, killed by some mysterious person. Then the light flashed on by the bed and glinted gold off his blonde hair. Anne felt the tension evaporate to be replaced by a blaze of anger.

"Leigh! What are you doing here?"

"Shuuush. Do you want to wake the whole house?"

"I couldn't care less!" Anne snapped. She could feel herself shaking slightly even now. "How did you get in?"

He motioned to the veranda doors that stood wide open.

Anne squinted at her ex-husband as he flashed her a wolfish grin. Leigh didn't look like he was well. Not well at all. He had always been tall, blonde and handsome; now it seemed like his health had been deteriorating.

"So you're here and you got in. How did you know where I'd be? And why not wait until morning like any sane person? It must be three o'clock!"

"Three-thirty," he stated succinctly. "I had to see you. I was there in the bushes when you first arrived, but I was afraid that you wouldn't talk to me. You refused to after the divorce."

Anne remembered the bitter anguish of two years ago. It seemed like the only true thing Leigh would tell her tonight.

"I wanted to come back – for old times' sake. We meant so much to each other and we could again." He watched from under his strange hooded eyelids, as though gauging the effect of his appeal to "auld lang syne." He must have found something encouraging since he finished up with, "I never forgot you."

"Especially now that I will inherit Islamorada. Who told you, by the way? Who told you about that?" Her voice rose stridently.

"Be still!" His tone changed to a low growl. As though remembering the role he had to play, he looked innocent. "Nobody told me anything. Why should they? I don't know any of the people down here. I've just been hanging out, watching and listening."

"And spying?' Anne gave him a genuine look of disgust. Someone close had contacted him for some hidden purpose.

"What do you want? Money? As usual?"

"Honey!" His voice sounded pained, as though finding it impossible to believe someone could judge him so harshly. He gave her the same slanty-eyed look he'd used many times as an actor on stage. Anne treated him to her best level-eyed glare, the one she reserved as business manager for customers in the photography shop who welshed on their bills after the pictures of their little darling had been taken and processed.

"As a matter of fact, I do need a little cash. The flight into Miami cost a lot more than I planned. And I still need a place to stay. Unless you'd like to put me up here?"

"Don't be a fool! You know how my grandfather feels about you. And he's not terribly forgiving, the way I am!"

"How is the old boy?" A speculative expression appeared in his gaze.

"He'll be alive for another hundred years!" But some of the fear sounded in her voice; Anne could never have passed for an actress. Leigh laughed and reached out. She jerked back and got out of bed, moving across the room, away from him and all the evil he represented.

"You never were a good liar. And it puts you at such a disadvantage when dealing with a person like me!" His eyes lit up when she reached for her purse.

"And you always will have a filthy mind." Anne held up five hundred dollar bills from her purse, just out of his reach. "Tell me one thing, Leigh. Honestly, if that's possible. I should get some kind of return for my money."

His gaze shifted from the bills to her face.

"What do you want to know?"

110

Anne watched his reaction closely. "Did you follow me to Orlando yesterday?"

He looked blank before his eyes turned crafty; he could have easily won an Academy Award a long time ago had he been acting. Suddenly Anne wanted nothing except for him to leave. She dropped the bills and walked out on the veranda. She'd tried for months to forgive him his indiscretions, feeling it only charitable to give her husband a second chance. Perfection did not exist. She knew this, but he'd thrown her charity back into her face.

Leigh scrambled to pick up the money behind her.

"I knew you'd help me out! You always did."

"Oblige me by leaving. And don't come back here again!"

"What's the matter?" And he spun around slowly, cautiously, away from the railing. "Aren't I good enough for you anymore? Things have certainly changed since the last time I came here. You begged me to get you out of this house, out of Key West for that matter!"

He grasped her arm and dragged her back toward the bed, a strange light in his eyes.

Anne felt the pulse hammering at her throat. Rape and then murder? Leigh yanked her arm into a hammerlock behind her back as she grasped the lighter on the night table. As she slammed the hard end into his eye, Leigh howled and jumped back.

Anne felt the pulse hammering at her throat.

"Get out of here. I'm not going to say it again! Before somebody sees us both." She stopped at the doorway, breathing heavily.

Leigh rubbed his face, which now sported a jagged black and blue slash. "If my face is marked, I'm through on the screen! If I'm scarred…"

At precisely that moment, they both heard the noise. Something creaked as though a person who had been lying still had had to change position.

Leigh didn't even stop to look around; he slithered to the veranda railing, lowered himself over the side and dropped the ten feet or so to the ground. As he disappeared through the rhododendrons, his ex-wife breathed a sigh of relief.

Anne's relief evaporated; she felt eyes boring into her. Shuddering involuntarily, she stepped hurriedly back into the room and locked the door before carefully pulling the drapes over the windows and creeping back to bed. A feeling of malevolence ebbed out of somewhere; its tendrils crept around her. Anne lay still for a long time, staring at the ceiling before finally falling back to sleep.

Chapter Thirteen

"A phantom ship, with each mast and spar
Across the moon like a prison bar,
And a huge black hulk, that was magnified
By its own reflection in the tide."
　　　　　　Paul Revere's Ride (Longfellow)

The following day dawned clear, without a cloud to mar the turquoise-speckled surface of the sky. Anne dressed, picked up her camera bag, and firmly pushed all thoughts of her ex-husband aside. Leigh appeared as an additional complication at Islamorada; she knew him to be crafty, unpredictable, and as uncontrollable as the tide swirling upon the rock-strewn beach. Now that he had gotten some money, he would stay out of the way or better yet, move on to greener pastures. Or so she hoped.

Anne got downstairs just in time to see Robin and Jack Cole driving up the road, past the row of flaming Poinciana trees, before reaching Route 1. Robin had been laughing at something the man had said right before they disappeared from sight. A certain similarity existed between Jack Cole and Leigh Giddings; Anne wished Robin would find a new interest since anyone would be better than the young diver from the *San Pedro*.

She turned toward the breakfast nook and walked right into Alex Stryker. He and Colin had evidently been waiting for her to come down.

Colin's face lit up.

113

"Mr. Stryker's only been here a few seconds. I persuaded him to have a cup of coffee while he waited."

As Anne slid into the nearest chair which Stryker held for her, she saw Tisha hovering in the doorway. She turned to bring in the coffee pot.

Stryker had chosen the chair directly across from her; the man was turning the cup in front of him round and round, not fidgeting exactly, since the movements were slow and very controlled. Suddenly he raised his eyes and gave her a long, deliberate stare.

Anne began chattering aimlessly in an effort to cover her nervousness.

"I was just thinking that it would be good publicity for the search on the *San Pedro* if I contacted one of the local papers to get some of these pictures printed."

Stryker laughed.

"Devlin is way ahead of you. He's already arranged a complete layout in the *Miami Herald* and the *Miami Daily News*, plus *The Times of Tampa*. Roger is usually short of money, and he's figuring the extra publicity might bring some speculators with cash that would come in handy."

Anne sipped at her coffee cautiously and buttered a roll. This could be an all-day expedition and it seemed better not to go hungry.

Colin frowned.

"There haven't been any more accidents out there? I wouldn't want Anne to have problems." David Gordon's chief trouble-shooter tried to be nonchalant, but Anne detected the urgency behind the question.

"Oh, I'll be staying around," Stryker said almost airily, "and Anne ought to be safe."

"Thanks," she commented dryly. "That makes me feel much easier."

She finished the coffee and rose. Stryker followed with the camera bag while Colin saw them to the door.

"Take care of yourself," Colin said again. He seemed worried.

Anne hadn't said anything about the trip yesterday to Water World; could it be that Colin knew something concerning today's expedition aboard the *Riga?* The thought appeared to be an uncomfortable one. Anne had known Colin Grant for years and admired him enormously; it frightened her to think he might be involved in the murders of the divers.

Stryker watched them with an odd expression on his face. Anne realized that she had been standing poised on the front veranda steps, frozen as though on film. His brows rose quizzically as he said, "Shall we go?" and turned to walk through the flowering garden and down toward the wharf.

When Anne looked back to wave at Colin, her attention focused on the upstairs window. She noticed a faint movement of the curtains as though someone had been standing there and had drawn suddenly back.

"I brought the whaler in," Stryker was saying. "It's not that long a ride out to the *Riga.* "

The grass ended abruptly and they moved across the sand. The brilliance of the sun reflected off the whiteness, making an almost inhuman glare. Anne reached for the sunglasses she had automatically tossed into her purse.

"Who will be aboard the *Riga* now? The regulars, I mean. Not the movie company or Colin."

"There's me, naturally. And Devlin. He comes and goes depending on where the action is. Jack Cole is the

115

same. You saw Squirrel the first night and we have two other divers besides, her brother and another girl who is a local and just hired on a couple of weeks ago. People aren't eager to work for Devlin. Not at all."

He helped her into the whaler and a moment later the small boat pulled away from shore.

"Do you think that business about a curse is turning everyone off?" Anne had to shout to be heard above the noise of the wind and motor. "And what about the accidents?"

"Has to be," Alex Stryker bellowed back. "Normally there are plenty of divers, hanging out in Sloppy Joe's place or even on the beach. But nobody has been rushing to sign up. Not since the first diver died."

Anne knew that Sloppy Joe's had been the haunt frequented by the late Ernest Hemingway; young men patronized the place, looking for work. If Devlin couldn't find help there, he had a big problem.

"What are you going to do?"

"Bring people in from the outside. That's one reason Devlin is interested in your taking pictures. We need all the good publicity we can get."

Conversation became impossible due to the noise. Anne sat back and let the wind tear through her silky hair. To the rear, Islamorada grew smaller in the distance; the high Spanish-styled house with its turret windows faded from sight, to be replaced by nothing but sea and sky. A sunlit glare reflected off of the water, as a tiny, black speck slowly materialized directly ahead.

"The *Riga*," Stryker shouted to make himself heard. "We'll be there in a few minutes."

Directly beyond the old minesweeper Anne saw the white, serpentine trough where the waves broke over the reef. Soon Stryker had maneuvered the whaler alongside the vessel; Anne climbed out of the smaller boat, up the accommodation ladder, and clambered over the gunwale. Stryker followed, carrying her camera bag as though it were made of fine china. Roger Devlin waited to greet them on the foredeck.

He held out a hand in welcome. "Delighted to have you aboard for the day."

"I understand that photographs of your operation here might be helpful, and it is my grandfather's dream to see the *San Pedro* completely salvaged. Let's just say that this is my contribution to the team effort." Her gaze wandered over the deck. "I notice that you're not far off the reef. Is this a particularly good location to look for treasure?"

Devlin ran his fingers through his hair. His sharp, black eyes appeared watchful; if someone had been attempting to sabotage the treasure-hunting expedition, they would have to be good indeed to manage to work around Roger Devlin. Anne could easily see the man in another age, decked out as a pirate and robbing the Spanish ships, much as the Dutch had done throughout the Caribbean area. He didn't have the well-defined good looks of the actor Paul Henreid in the movie the *Spanish Main*, yet he did remind her of someone. Anne's mind turned somersaults thinking of all the people here in Key West. Yes, he resembled Colin Grant, only where Colin's job made him a troubleshooter on land, Devlin's salvage operation made him one on the water.

"To answer your question, Spain customarily sent one convoy of ships per year to-and-from the New World. They had a regular route all mapped out, called Carrera de Indias. The *San Pedro* had been a part of this

117

ship caravan, the flagship bringing up the rear. The group sailed from Havana and ran into a nasty blowup off the Keys. The *San Pedro* seems to have gotten the worst of it and she went down, along with two others. The rest of the fleet limped back into Havana Harbor to wait for the following year, but earlier in the season."

Anne's eyes traveled over the different types of equipment spread out on the deck; the pile-up formed a small-sized mountain.

"Was there so much to salvage? It must take an unearthly amount of money to man an operation like this one."

"It does," Devlin spoke wryly. "That's why we're hoping these photographs of yours will bring in more capital."

"Okay. I'm convinced. Just let me get a couple of pictures of the wheelhouse and foredeck from this angle." Anne reached down, carefully removed her Nikon from the camera bag, focused the lens and took several shots of the deck area. Looking up, she nodded to Devlin; he turned and led the way across the foredeck past a winch and a shark repellant cage and inside, away from the sun. Stryker brought up the rear as they went through a companionway on the starboard side of the *Riga* and entered the wheelhouse. Then they were on the bridge where a multitude of different instruments met her gaze.

Anne's first reaction to what Devlin showed her consisted of amazement; she had no idea that the old minesweeper would be quite so complicated. Her experience in regard to vessels consisted in operating an outboard on a dingy or a whaler, but the *Riga* seemed to be a full-fledged ocean-going ship. Anne had a feeling that her knowledge about outboards and even diving was going to turn out to be minimal in the extreme.

Her feeling of inadequacy increased as Devlin, accompanied always by Stryker, showed off the entire vessel, from the forepeak to the stern deck. Anne's lingering impression was that no amount of money had been spared to give the *Riga* every luxury imaginable. If the ex-minesweeper didn't find treasure, it wasn't because someone hadn't done a first rate job of decking the ship out like a floating palace in the *Arabian Nights*.

They continued through the luxurious for'ard salon to the after-cabin, which reminded Anne of a floating laboratory, complete, naturally enough, with just about everything a laboratory ought to have. They proceeded past the sleeping quarters to the engine room, where Devlin expounded on the engine for a time and Anne dutifully took photos in triplicate. A room designated as the treasure room turned into a real bonanza; Devlin told her a little about it as he fumbled opening the lock.

"We had problems finding the treasure originally, not just because the *San Pedro* broke into so many pieces after she hit the reef, but because of the records back in Seville. She was like a ghostly, phantom ship. We just couldn't pin her down!"

"What did the records say?"

"That this galleon had gone aground on one of the Keys north of here. Somewhere! But the Spaniards had an interesting system of calling the Keys by more than one name. When you think there are over ten thousand of them, life gets complicated."

"But if the cargo is so scattered, how do you find things? Do you just search everywhere?"

119

"No, we have a magnetometer, a metal detector. We chart a course and criss-cross off a particular area of ocean. The whole process is called magging. Anyway, every time the magnetometer shows something, we toss a buoy over the side and afterward go back to dive on it. That's what everyone is doing now. Diving. There's nobody on board except the three of us."

"On certain days," Alex added, "we only dive once or twice. On others, it's thirty or forty times."

Devlin's key finally opened the lock after he jiggled it around for several moments. With a dramatic flourish, similar to Houdini pulling a rabbit out of a hat, he opened the door and entered.

Anne had never seen so much metal in her entire life. When she mentioned this to Stryker, he just grinned and pointed out that there was a good deal more besides; at Islamorada and at the bank in Key West under guard.

Anne spotted five cannon, heavily encrusted with dried crustaceans from being buried in the sea.

"Are these gold?" she asked Devlin, running a finger over the surface of the nearest gun.

"Uh-uh. Bronze. And hard to find. Bronze doesn't record on the metal detector. Finding it is just a matter of luck."

"Look at the coins, too," Devlin insisted. Anne did, peering into the glass. She could make out the portraits of Ferdinand and Isabella of Spain on one, but tarnish obscured the images on the others.

Finally, she saw the jewelry, beautiful, long golden filigree chains, delicate and airy. A cross, inlaid with rubies and emeralds had likely been worn as a decoration by the Spanish nobility.

After Anne had run through another roll of film, the three of them moved out the door. Devlin carefully locked up his treasure and they ambled back to the main salon. As Stryker poured drinks for all, Anne asked a question that had been bothering her ever since she'd seen the treasure below decks.

"Tell me, Mr. Devlin, why are you keeping most of the salvaged items here? Why not in the banks in Miami or Key West? It would be safer."

Devlin patiently worded his reply. "I don't trust banks. Never have, never will. And the way people feel about treasure, if it were kept in a vault, somebody would try to get it. It's better here on the *Riga*. Nobody can come on board without making the trip over the water and one of the divers is always on site."

Anne hesitated to mention that it was possibly one of these same divers who had killed two people and would hardly even pause at a spot of straight robbery. She grimaced at her most uncomfortable thoughts.

Stryker spoke up. "If you'd like to go down to the wreck site, we've got all the equipment on board and..."

"No! I mean no thanks. I'd rather not."

A long silence ensued as Stryker studied her.

"Look, if you're worried about the dive site, it's only fifteen feet or so below the surface. There wouldn't be any decompression or..."

"It's not the dive site," Anne broke in hurriedly. "My brother, my twin brother, got himself killed in a scuba accident five years ago down on the beach by Islamorada. His body hasn't ever been recovered. I haven't felt like diving since."

"I can see how something like that would turn you off. But it would be very safe. Nothing could go wrong."

121

"Why are you so insistent? What difference does it make to you?" For the smallest fraction of a second, an image formed in her mind, unbidden, of a diver slowly strangling to death due to a malfunctioning regulator.

Stryker didn't seem to notice anything amiss. "I'm just trying to get better acquainted although it is a bit of an uphill struggle, if you don't mind my saying so."

Anne could feel the indecision that must be written all over her face, but as she stared at Stryker, the mental picture of the diver faded. Her acquiescence must have been obvious.

"Good! I knew you'd have the guts to go. You'll get some first-hand information about the site and maybe even see the other divers, if they should find more gold."

"All right, Alex." She did want to dive again, to feel the cool greenness of the water slithering up against her flesh, almost like a second skin.

"Now that it's settled, I'll see about the equipment," Roger Devlin put in. He left.

Anne leaned back against the wall; she forgot about Stryker and tried to think. The time seemed long overdue for her to forgive herself. By going back into the ocean, perhaps she could erase the memories of that fateful day five years ago. Only by returning to the scene of the accident could a true cure be effected.

Stryker continued speaking. "Don't worry, Anne. It will be fine. I'll see to it, personally. You'll have a great time. I promise."

He reached for her hand and held it. As his warm confidence seeped into her, Anne knew that he had spoken the truth.

Everything would be just fine.

Chapter Fourteen

"The chameleon may change its color
But it is the chameleon still."

(Shakespeare)

Anne shoved herself off of the side of the whaler and plunged downward, following Alex Stryker into the greenish-blue depths of the ocean below. The current tugged at her legs as she descended, the sea water closing over her head in a swarthy swirl of foam. Exhaling sharply while simultaneously pressing down hard on the top of the scuba mask cleared it of water. Air bubbles trailed back to the surface. Inhaling slowly, Anne drifted ever downward in a spiral, keeping Stryker in her sight. The only sound that broke the eerie silence of the descent was a hollow rasping of her breath, in and out, through the regulator mouthpiece. Now the water changed color, from the reddish-yellow of the surface to the green fluorescent shade of the depths. Anne looked around, trying to see in all directions at once. Glancing down, she noted a school of incandescent yellow grunts; they seemed like little lights flashing on-and-off close by.

Still Anne and Stryker descended. She tilted her head back, cleared her face mask again and swallowed twice to relieve the pressure on her ears. The world seemed all blue. She and Alex floated about ten feet down into the sea; the reds, yellows and oranges had been ferreted out farther up. Many holes in the sand had

123

probably been made by the divers; obviously this area had been thoroughly searched at one time or another. Anne noticed Alex beckoning to her. She swam over and with her eyes followed his pointing finger. Two things appeared simultaneously; the reef and the divers from the *Riga* digging in the sand.

Two black-garbed figures worked in full scuba gear. Anne thought she recognized Squirrel, but underwater, everyone looked very much alike. The divers used an air gun that sucked up the sand off the bottom of the ocean at a terrific rate of speed, making a large hole. Unfortunately, no silver or gold appeared.

Eventually, Anne kicked hard with her fins, crossing in front of Alex. They swam farther. When he suddenly stopped, Anne almost collided with him.

Directly in their path appeared a leopard ray, moving slowly through the sea grasses; the midnight black ray marked with rings of white on his body. They froze as it swam closer. Anne glanced up toward the surface, but knew better than to move. At the last moment, the ray turned aside; as it passed overhead, she could see the poisonous stinger inside its tail along with the darts that could do an infinite amount of damage to man or fish.

Anne exhaled sharply once the danger vanished; she had been subconsciously holding her breath. Alex looked around and then he proceeded upward at a sharp angle toward the reef. As Anne turned to follow, she spotted a movement of something far to her left. She swung around, her eyes searching the depths. The blue-black of the water pressed down everywhere. Anne could feel eyes boring into her. A fish perhaps? Shark? She could feel the sweat breaking out all over her and felt frozen like a mummy in an underwater tomb. And then something brushed up against her shoulder; Stryker swung into her line of sight, a question in his eyes. Anne shook her head. Shrugging slightly, she stepped back, feeling a fool. Her overactive imagination had paralyzed her again; she beckoned to Stryker to move forward as they both paddled up toward the reef.

Anne forgot about everything else as a mirage of flashing color met her eyes. She felt like she moved through a wonderland of magentas, scarlets, and geranium shades which seemed to whirl and ebb like fallen leaves dancing in a wind of underwater currents, as the wonders of the depths paraded before them. The fish ignored the two divers; Anne and Alex might as well not have existed for all the attention they received.

Anne saw Stryker beckon peremptorily to her; she caught up and looked to where he pointed, close to some undulating sea fans and into a crevasse in the ocean bottom. Then she spotted a silvery flash of light that seemed like the blade of a knife passing through the water. Only it wasn't a knife, but a barracuda; Alex Stryker saw him at exactly the same moment.

He put out a hand to warn Anne away; she could feel the jolt as his fingers touched her, almost like electricity passing through her skin. Anne looked into the face behind the diving mask; he had felt it, too.

Stryker moved closer, his hands gently touching Anne's shoulder. She could feel her breathing stop in her throat as he turned her carefully around to face him; then he gently pulled both regulators from their mouths and kissed her. The water swirled in waves of white foam around them as their lips met under the cool green surface. He stopped, his eyes searching hers. Anne wound her arms around his neck and pulled him closer to her for a last embrace.

Then their air had vanished and both reached for the regulators at the same moment. Stryker linked arms with her as they traveled slowly upward toward the surface, spiraling around, almost like two tops spinning in the vortex of the greenish water.

Anne felt giddy like she was in free-fall; her earlier suspicions of Stryker seemed to have been put on hold. "I don't think he's the murderer. He can't be! I couldn't feel this way about him otherwise."

And then their two heads broke the surface of the serpent sea as they scrambled to drag themselves back on board the whaler.

Anne shed her scuba tank, yanked the regulator out of her mouth and pulled off the scuba mask, dropping it in the bottom of the small boat. Stryker duplicated her actions before turning and gently pulling Anne into his arms. He smoothed her hair back from her forehead, gray eyes dark with passion and longing for her. When he spoke, his voice seemed unsteady.

"Well, Anne, what do you think? Was it like you remembered?"

Anne rested her head on his chest.

"It's glorious. Even better than I thought it would be." Her eyes went to the sky; two blue herons circled overhead, round and round. She saw a silver flash as one dived down and pulled a fish out of the water.

"We need to get back. Devlin will think there's been some sort of mishap. But...I'd really just like to stand and hold you forever." Stryker planted a last kiss, warm and inviting, on her mouth before starting the outboard motor and turning the whaler toward the *Riga*.

Seeing the dive ship, Anne attempted to marshal her thoughts as her mind returned to the most pressing problem of identifying the murderer. The time underwater allowed her to forget momentarily, but now she quickly woke up to reality.

Alex watched as he maneuvered the whaler. He finally spoke up.

"You're so quiet. Didn't you have a good time?"

"It's beautiful, but…"

But you can't forget about the other night when your mysterious visitor hit you over the head at the tree house."

Wordlessly, Anne nodded. What had been behind the attack? Had it been the man who had been following her? Or possibly her ex-husband? Leigh's presence here could be accounted for in many ways, but accidently wasn't one of them.

As they came alongside the *Riga* Alex continued speaking. "Have dinner with me tonight, Anne. I've got to talk to you about what's happened. I can't very well do it today, not with Roger here. But what I have to say could be vital – to both of us."

Anne studied him carefully. But wasn't this what she wanted, part of the reason she remained in Key West – a chance to find out what was actually going on?

"Okay. I can drop my film off on the way into Key West. I'd like to talk to you, too."

The whaler bounced through the waves and reached the side of the *Riga.* As Devlin helped her over the gunwale, Anne convinced herself that she had accepted the invitation because of the valid information that Stryker might be persuaded to divulge. Yet she knew that wasn't entirely true. Stryker…she had been attracted to him since their first meeting on the beach. But yet...things seemed to be getting more, rather than less, complicated!

Anne discovered that she had trouble concentrating on Roger Devlin as he continued telling her about the instrumentation advances on board the dive ship. Catching Stryker's eye, Anne had the feeling that he had the same problem. She found herself eagerly anticipating an unusual evening, a night to remember. Anne knew Stryker would definitely not be a disappointment; she felt it in her soul.

>>>>*Gordon*<<<<

Stryker took Anne to the Pier House Restaurant that night, where waiters hovered over the two of them, anxious to serve. As they sat there eating lobster, the pair watched the dredged turquoise of the sky change to a deep mauve as the sun sank into the sea. At last, even the mauve turned to gun-metal gray and then black.

They had been quiet for a number of minutes, sitting peacefully at their window table, but the silence felt very comfortable. Alex glanced up suddenly. Anne paused and said the first thing that came into her mind.

"Do you think there is something behind these accidents – a motive, so to speak?"

Stryker turned his water glass round and round in front of him; it seemed to be a habit of his.

"I'm positive of it. Somebody is trying to sabotage the wreck site. There have been too many odd occurrences. Two divers lost, both of them professionals. How obvious can it be?"

"Had either of them been having any problems? People react oddly underwater if they're under stress."

"I checked. Devlin told me that Adams acted kind of strange before the dive. But they'd been in a hurry, so he let him go down anyway."

"What about the other diver?"

"There was no obvious reason for him to die. The water wasn't that deep. I checked myself. He could have made it to the surface easily."

"Maybe he panicked."

"Yeah. Maybe." Stryker sounded unconvinced.

"It could fit in with what's happened to me." Anne told him about her feeling of being followed the day before. "Not to mention being hit on the head!"

"Can you think of any reason for it?"

A mental picture of Leigh flashed into her head, but she answered Stryker's question with a firm no. He glanced inquiringly at her as she kept talking.

"There's still the light in the tree house, too. Who's been using it? And why?"

"That *why*," he repeated softly. "That's what's bothering me. Why should anyone want to stop the treasure hunt? What possible reason could there be?"

"Maybe an enemy of my grandfather. Or Colin's. Trying to get back at them. If not, then I don't know. There's the movie company, too. Although what it could have to do with them, I can't imagine."

"You know, I asked you out to forget about all of this tonight. Instead we seem to have spent the entire time raking it up."

"All right. No more, at least for this evening."

"I have a great idea. Have you ever been to the southernmost point in the United States?"

"You mean here on Key West? Not recently."

Stryker got up and paid the bill before they walked out toward the parking lot.

"Let's go down there. There's a legend that says if you get sand in your shoes from that shore, you're doomed to return to the Keys."

"Alex, you're a romantic! Do you really believe it?"

"Let's say I haven't made up my mind."

The cool air, like a soulful breeze, brushed against them. Anne breathed in deeply. The rest of the day had vanished along with the sun; she could hardly see the dark outline of the palmettos against the night sky.

Alex went to collect the car; the restaurant's location was right across the street from the Conch Tour Train stop. The place appeared deserted at this hour and would remain so until the following morning; it had a lonely, forlorn feeling about it, as though the site had been abandoned. Anne scurried eagerly into the car as soon as Alex stopped.

They drove through the main part of the town, past innumerable shops, cafes, and finally Hemingway's historic Sloppy Joe's establishment. Anne noted young couples wandering around hand in hand; on this sort of night, it was hardly surprising.

She leaned back against the leather seat of Alex's classic Stingray and tried to relax. He drove rapidly, but radiated competence that made the speed unimportant. Given the opportunity, Anne studied him in the half-light; strong, full of determination, he reminded her of Colin Grant and her grandfather.

Stryker pulled the car up to the pier. Anne saw the inevitable sign, announcing to one and all that this was the southernmost point of the United States, in case a tourist existed who didn't already know. They got out of the car, ignored the sign and meandered slowly toward the milky, white-skirted water. Looking down at the ocean from the pier, Anne watched the undertow suck against the wooden structure, seeking to pull the whole thing into the sea.

Alex leaned on the railing and appeared to study the lacey waves as they rose and fell beneath them. Without any prompting, he began to talk; he told her about his childhood in White Sulphur Springs, Montana, where his father had owned a ranch. His mother died when he'd been a child and Alex had run wild, growing up around the ranch hands, learning how to rope and ride with the best of them. His religion consisted of the wide open prairie; his education in managing a ranch. When his father died, Alex discovered that his home had been mortgaged to the hilt, along with every steer and horse on the spread; nothing remained by the time all the bills had been paid. Feeling betrayed by everyone, Stryker wandered west to California, only to find a plastic society that did not inspire him to stay. So he came East and then south to Florida.

"But why Key West? Why did you settle here?" Anne's curiosity ran rampant.

Stryker shrugged. "I'd been in Miami, but I wanted to get out for a bit. I think I'm just a country boy at heart."

"What did you do in Miami?"

"A little bit of everything." Stryker spoke evasively. "I always kept moving. This is the longest I've been settled for some time. But tell me about yourself. How did you happen to be here?"

"It's an ordinary enough story. I grew up in New York, spent summers on the Keys, went to college." She hesitated, "And you've heard about Edward. I'd gotten married, but it didn't work out. I landed in California, but after my divorce, I returned to Cedar Key here in Florida and opened an art/photography studio with a friend, Cristel Slivka. That's what I'll be going back to eventually when all of this," Anne gestured vaguely, thinking of the accidents that weren't accidents at all, "is over."

"Your grandfather could live for years, yet, Anne."

"I wasn't thinking about him so much as about Leigh, my ex-husband. He's down here, slithering around in the bushes like some kind of snake."

"I hadn't heard." He spoke slowly, lingering over each word as though it held a special significance.

"Like a bad penny. I was just getting over him, too. But he knows about my grandfather's will being changed and that Islamorada will be mine. Don't ask me how, but he knows."

"And that's why he showed up?"

She nodded. Anne leaned back against the railing and stared for a moment at the star-sequined sky, feeling as alone as she had years before, when she'd realized that Leigh had married her not out of love but for her money.

Stryker seemed to understand her feeling; suddenly his arms wrapped around her, warm and safe and very comfortable.

"Your hair is wet from the spray." His hands smoothed back the errant strands.

Anne wound her arms around his neck; she felt his breath, soft and sweet on her throat. His touch made her feel so fulfilled, so alive. She had begun living here, on this beach at the southernmost point of the United States.

Stryker's breathing quickened. But then he paused and turned slowly away.

"What is it, Alex?"

"I think I'm falling in love with you. But…there is something you should know. Something I can't tell you – at least not now."

Anne studied him. Several long moments passed.

"All right, Alex. But…I had a wonderful time. And when you're ready to tell me about whatever it is, I'll be waiting."

Stryker pulled his gaze away. His face had set as he turned and escorted Anne back to the Stingray. They both remained silent until the gates of Islamorada came into view.

Chapter Fifteen

"He'll sit in a barn, And keep himself warm,
And hide his head under his wing, Poor thing!"
— *Mother Goose Nursery Rhymes* (The Robin)

Alex drove the Corvette up to the entrance of Gordon Hall. It was late, very — very late that same night; he turned quickly to Anne, his eyes dark with desire as he studied her face, seeking to memorize every detail.

"Be careful, my love. *For me!* I don't think I could stand it if anything happened to you now."

"Do take care, Alex." Anne hesitated then climbed slowly out of the car. Everything had changed in the space of one evening; she felt her world would never be the same. Not now, not since Alex Stryker had entered it.

She watched silently as the car pulled away; she saw the glimmer of shuttered headlights as Alex parked the car at Little Isle and returned in the whaler to the *Riga*. The lights from the boat winked on and off like miniature beacons as he sent it over the waves. When Anne turned and opened the heavy front door, she walked in on the ugliest scene she had yet encountered since coming home.

Robin stood white-faced, her back to the high marble fireplace and the table with the dead stuffed birds; she looked pale as if she might collapse at any second. Across from her, speaking from his wheelchair, sat David Gordon. Maud stood behind him, dressed in her shroudal black. She reminded Anne of a vulture hovering over a kill, waiting for the lion to leave before moving in.

The room was silent before David Gordon's voice lashed out, a low tone rather like the snap of a whip as he played it over Robin. It reminded Anne of another occasion long ago when he had spoken in just such a manner to her, where there had been no sorrow, no forgiveness, regardless of how much she had pleaded.

"This whole business has been a disgrace from start to finish. And now you talk of leaving Islamorada, after chasing that diver all over the Keys. Well, I've warned you before and I'll say it again. Leave and you'll do it without one cent from me. I'll cut you out of my will completely, that's what I'll do!" The old man sat back, a look of satisfaction on his face.

Robin seemed to have recovered her voice.

"Couldn't you at least try and get to know Jack a little bit better before you condemn him? He's the man I've waited for all my life!"

David Gordon ignored her words as though they had never been spoken. "Drag the Gordon name through the mud, will you? I won't stand for it! Not again!"

Anne jumped from her position by the door.

David Gordon repeated, "I won't stand by to have us insulted. Do you understand?"

A smile flitted over Maud's face. It broke the trance; Anne covered the room to Robin's side at amazing speed.

"I'm sure you've made yourself plain enough. Robin would never have deliberately disgraced the family name."

"Stay out of this, Anne. You're not in a position to say much of anything. Not after the disaster you made of your own life!"

"Leigh loved me! At least in the beginning!"

"And where is he? Another low-life, just like this Cole fellow. I'm beginning to think you are two of a kind. If you think you'll be better off away from Islamorada, go! I won't stop you – either of you!" He glowered, his eyes flickering back and forth between the pair of them. And then his body shuddered and contracted in a rictus of pain that almost doubled him over.

"Now see what you've done!" Maud hissed her satisfaction over Robin's bent and chastened head. As Anne tried to move to her grandfather's side, he waved her away in disgust.

"Help me upstairs, Sister. These two deserve each other!"

As Maud moved to obey, she gave Anne a triumphant look. The two moved slowly upstairs, leaving Anne alone with a sobbing, inconsolable Robin.

<<<<Gordon>>>>

The following day dawned crystal bright with none of the storm clouds from the previous evening. Anne saw her grandfather at lunch; the photographs of the dive site had been printed in the local papers and in Miami, too, generating new interest and also two backers with available cash, putting the old man in a fine humor. It seemed as though the cut and parry of the night before had never been. In a way, Anne felt grateful for this small favor.

She tried to call her business partner, Cristel Slivka, to advise her that she would not be returning to Cedar

Key immediately. The only response available came from the answering machine. Anne shrugged. Perhaps Cristel had gone out to take photographs or drum up business, or perhaps she'd stayed in the back of the shop to work on her jewelry designs. Her partner would hardly be sitting on her hands with the entire store to manage. Anne left a detailed message, asked that Cristel call if there seemed to be trouble, and went back to worrying about the who and why of the sabotaged dive site.

Walking away from the telephone on the hall landing, Anne trailed back into the main room. She spotted Colin Grant and although she tried to be quiet, one of the stairs creaked and shifted as she passed down the flight. Colin stirred; a glimmer of apparent apprehension appeared on his face. Then he recognized her and his expression changed imperceptibly. Anne might have almost imagined the look of fear as she approached.

"I haven't been seeing too much of you these days. Business in Miami and all."

"Please, Colin. Nobody has to explain to me about my grandfather. I've known him for ages. He didn't make millions of dollars in industry by being easy to work for." She went over to the elaborate, hand-carved liquor cabinet next to the bar and poured two small glasses of sherry.

"Have a drink. You'll feel better."

The silence lingered into several minutes before either of them spoke again.

"They're still having trouble at the dive site. Devlin was over this morning telling me about it. Things seem peaceful and suddenly trouble breaks out for no apparent reason."

Anne leaned back into one of the chairs near the fireplace.

"What sort of trouble?"

"All kinds. We hired three more divers. There are frequent malfunctions with equipment. You'd think," his mouth twisted bitterly, "that Devlin would be able to pin it down. But no, he claims he has no idea who is responsible. Of course," and here he blurted out what had really been on his mind, "it might be Devlin himself!"

Anne's head jerked upward.

"Devlin? Why on earth would he sabotage his own dive site?"

Colin sighed. "I don't know. Unless somebody is paying him off. Your grandfather has a lot of enemies and there's no question about it. Maybe somebody is using this as a way to get even." He hesitated. "And if having two people killed isn't enough, our mysterious killer is writing cute little letters as warnings. Look at these."

He pulled a crumpled piece of paper from his pocket. On it were words cut from a newspaper.

"Stay off the *San Pedro* or someone else will die!" On the bottom appeared a picture of a skull and crossbones, common among the pirates of ages past.

Anne fingered the note.

"Corny."

"But oh, so effective! Everyone is nervous, waiting for the next incident." He twisted the paper savagely in his hand. "And there isn't anything corny in the accidents that we've been having. I'm not a superstitious man, but I'm beginning to wonder if there might not be something in this curse business."

"You know that's ridiculous, Colin. A person wrote this message, not some sinister spirit from the Dark Ages. You've told the police, I suppose?"

"Yes, after the first one." He noticed her surprised look. "This is the third letter, Anne. The police checked for fingerprints, which were nonexistent, naturally. The things come in the mail that Stryker or I pick up here daily."

"Stryker? He comes in?"

"Uh-huh. Devlin trusts him completely for some reason that escapes me."

She remained silent. So Stryker picked up the mail! Anne wondered that he hadn't stopped and asked about her. Although, in all honesty, she had been occupied with her grandfather's illness and worry about Robin and Jack Cole, but...her lips curved upward into a smile just thinking about their dinner together.

Colin rose and paced over to the window and back, restlessly.

"The thing is our backers are getting worried about their investment. Try telling them that these rumors are all a lot of superstitious nonsense. You want to go back in time, just try talking to the group of people underwriting this operation!"

Anne's attention returned to the present. "But I thought my grandfather had decided to finance the whole venture – or just about."

"No way! Do you have any idea what an effort like this on the *San Pedro* has cost so far? The remodeling of the *Riga* alone cost millions – plus all the equipment and salaries for the divers. I suppose your grandfather could have financed the project himself, but it seemed a better business investment to sell shares to different interested parties – which I did, following his instructions."

"Haven't they been getting their money's worth?"

"Yes. And it's a point I keep bringing up. But Devlin has big ideas and wants to send down even more divers. With all these rumors, there is a problem finding people who will have anything to do with the Spanish wreck."

Anne looked unhappy.

"Didn't the pictures and layout I just did for the newspaper help?"

Colin smiled.

"Of course. But we seem to be running into too many problems. That's all it is, hopefully."

Colin and Anne both turned as the sound of a car motor came to them. He picked up the briefcase he'd left lying on the table.

"I'm off." He hesitated. "Please be careful, Anne. These notes could be directed at any of us – even you."

"But why should anyone be interested in me?"

"Why should anyone want to stop the diving on the *San Pedro?* Just take care."

She waved as the car pulled down the driveway before turning back and leaning against the door frame. Colin's words were upsetting, along with those gruesome little notes. Their very simplicity made them seem far more dangerous than any kind of threat that could have been made.

Suddenly, Anne did not want to be in the house a moment longer; turning, she walked across the veranda and down toward the boathouse. She heard voices through the garden gate and saw a man and woman standing there. Diana Moon and Frank Blaine. Anne hadn't thought much about the movie people lately. They had expressed their concern about David Gordon, naturally, but for the most part, Peter James and Aldridge Thornton spent their time out on the *Riga,* supposedly getting the "atmosphere" for the movie, to direct and write, respectively. Diana and Frank stayed by themselves on most days, taking one of the many cars at Islamorada and driving into Key West. Diana seemed to have calmed down and reconsidered staying at Gordon Hall; there had been no more outbursts from her. Anne wondered if there had ever been anything to the woman's claims in the first place.

She avoided the cloying, scented garden and tramped steadily across the expanse of knee-high grasses to the beach. Pulling off her shoes, she moved toward the ocean, her feet making scrunchy noises in the grainy sand.

Islamorada seemed a mere dot in the distance. The estate and Gordon Hall had felt almost human to her at times, the house watching the sea for whatever might be cast up on the shore.

Anne smiled at this flight of fancy. Her eyes dropped to the sand and she froze into stillness. Footprints! They had begun a few yards back, but in her preoccupation with the notes and the problems at the dive site, she had ambled right over them without even really noticing.

The footprints ran in a line along the shore. The marks looked widespread, much farther apart than her own tracks. *Definitely a man or at least a tall woman*, she thought. Anne glanced back toward Islamorada; although she had wandered a long way from the house, the property still belonged to the estate. Technically, whoever walked here at the south end had been trespassing.

Be careful! It could be someone perfectly harmless, like a tramp beachcombing. But inside, Anne knew that this just wasn't the case. The prints had an ominous meaning, a connection with the events that had taken place during the past several weeks.

Islamorada had entirely disappeared from her sight. Nobody could be seen along the expanse of beach. Anne noted the chill in the air, despite the earlier humidity of the day. This section of the property seemed to be completely isolated from everywhere. The familiar egrets circling in the cerulean blue sky above provided the only movement.

Nobody would hear or see if something happened.

The tracks turned inward through some mangrove plants as Anne followed them doggedly onward. Swarms of mosquitoes buzzed around; she slapped at them angrily in vexation. But then the ground hardened and the tracks vanished, as quickly as they had first appeared.

The undergrowth thickened here; ferns surrounded the heavy oak and pine trees. Anne pushed ahead and felt something brush faintly up against her face. She jumped backward, thinking of snakes, but no, tendrils of Spanish moss dangled down, long and whitish from the branches.

Anne stopped to catch her breath, which literally seemed stuck in her throat. The undergrowth and shrubbery ahead moved, as though her unseen adversary had passed through seconds before. Anne twisted and turned, trying to see in all four directions at once. She saw a movement in the brush, so she stumbled in that direction, but nobody could be seen when she finally arrived.

Anne halted again, trying to get her bearings. Someone clearly didn't want to be recognized. She leaned back toward one of the pines; the fact that the person remained just out of sight indicated that they planned some nefarious activity. Otherwise, surely the individual would have come into the open by now.

Anne briefly toyed with the idea of going back to Islamorada and finding someone to help her look around. She had just convinced herself that this seemed to be the sanest course of action, when her attention turned to a movement in the woods. The movement blurred and the figure appeared indistinct; it looked like part of an arm wearing a dark blue coat. Then it vanished but someone had been there; at least Anne thought so.

She wound her way forward through the palmettos, zigzagging back and forth, trying to make as little noise as possible. The low grasses here swirled around her legs, reminiscent of the ocean floor with its waving ripples. Again, when she reached the place of movement, she saw nobody.

The person played a nasty little game; for what purpose, she couldn't begin to guess. Then Anne felt a touch on her arm; as the dark shrouded figure rose up directly behind her, she screamed and screamed again, shattering the stillness of the ocean air into a thousand miniscule pieces, before turning and trying to run.

Chapter Sixteen

"Unbidden guests Are often Welcomest
When they are gone."
King Henry the Sixth (Shakespeare)

"Anne, wait!" His arm reached out to stop her pell-mell flight into the bushes.

"Leigh!" She halted and snapped out his name in exasperated anger. Her ex-husband had materialized like somebody off of the Enterprise on *Star Trek*! "What are you doing crawling around in the brush?"

"I could ask you the same question. Actually, I was hanging around Gordon Hall and saw you walk down the beach. So I followed. But you stopped for awhile. That's when I cut ahead and kept on going."

"Those were your tracks that I saw?" She should have known, it was so typical of Leigh!

"Uh-huh. Actually, I wanted to have a talk with you. My sources of information tell me that the old man has gotten worse. And that the way his will is now, you stand to inherit the lot."

"Who's been telling you this? Someone's keeping you well-informed. Who is it?"

He smiled – a nasty cold-blooded smile.

"Actually, I've collected a number of juicy items you might like to know. Of course, I have a price!"

"Don't you always?" Anne felt very much older than her twenty-four years. Leigh, by contrast, looked much better than the last time she had seen him. The thought made her feel extremely depressed.

"What do you have to sell?" *Money*, she thought gloomily. *It always comes back to money.*

"Not so fast. We'll make a trade. You give me cash; I give you information."

"I won't buy blind, Leigh."

"You bring the money. Fifty thousand dollars. The day after tomorrow, Wednesday. I'll meet you at eleven in the boathouse off the wharf."

"Look, what's it about? And what makes you think I can get that much money?"

"With that lucrative little camera business of yours on Cedar Key? You grossed eighty-five thousand last year alone. Or go borrow it from your precious Grandfather Gordon. Or on your inheritance. I couldn't care less. It's your problem. Just bring me that money!"

The way he said her grandfather's name left no doubt how he felt concerning the Gordons. Anne wanted nothing more than to get away from him. She couldn't begin to understand how this man could have at one time been attractive to her.

"Get the cash! It will be worth it. All your questions will be answered!"

Anne studied him. He looked sly and secretive, but then he always looked sly and secretive. Maybe she should try and find out exactly what he thought he knew.

"Okay. Eleven on Wednesday."

"You're being smart. And remember to be on time. I won't wait!"

Anne turned to go, wanting only to escape.

"And you keep away from Islamorada," she threw back over her shoulder. "You know my grandfather. If anyone reports seeing you hanging around near the house, I don't know what he'll do." She could feel Leigh's eyes boring into her back. As soon as the trees provided an effective screen, she began to run.

It seemed like a dozen miles, but finally Islamorada came into sight. Anne stopped, panting; sweat seeped through to her blouse. What had just happened? She had a date with a man who might well be a murderer! But, perhaps not. Leigh fell into many categories, but he was not capable of killing anyone. He simply didn't have the guts to go through with it. Standing there, Anne felt almost dirty, thinking of his rotten blackmail scheme. She sat down and played back the whole scene with her ex-husband in her mind.

Something felt wrong about the whole thing. She examined every step, going over what had happened, reliving the events from seeing the footprints to finding Leigh amongst the palmettos. Then Anne knew. The arm she'd seen had been draped in a navy blue material, possibly serge. Leigh had had on light gray.

>>>>*Gordon*>>>>

Islamorada gleamed and glistened in the heat of the day, as Anne finally padded back to the garden and into the house, her feet making no noise on the heavy carpeting. Upstairs, Maud said in her usual acid tone that her brother slept and shouldn't be disturbed. Anne continued to her bedroom and found Jezebella curled comfortably up in the bed, her head resting on the pillow. The little cat looked up with her huge eyes and then went back to sleep. Anne felt tempted to join her, but was too restless to be still; she finally wandered downstairs to see Frank Blaine staring morosely out the front door.

Standing on the floor beside him four suitcases were stacked, one on top of the other. Peter James talked with him in a low undertone which ceased abruptly.

"Hello, Miss Gordon. How nice it is to be able to speak to you before I leave."

"Leave, Mr. Blaine? Is your work here finished?"

"We have overstayed our welcome quite a bit," P.J. put in. "Thornton has finished his screen play about the *San Pedro*. There just isn't too much more for Frank to do here. I'll be praying upon your hospitality for a few days, yet. And so will Diana."

Anne hadn't thought much about Diana Moon or the movie company in days. She had thought about the murders and about Alex Stryker, not necessarily in that order. Blaine seemed to feel it necessary to clarify the director's statement.

"Diana appears fascinated by Islamorada – spends most of her time down on the beach."

"I'm glad she's so satisfied."

The two men exchanged glances over her head. It confirmed that Diana's interest in Islamorada extended beyond the beach and looking at fish and flowers. Blaine had definitely been given his walking papers. Anne wondered whether Jack Cole or someone else had the actress' rapt attention. At any rate, Frank seemed to have struck out completely.

A long, black chauffeur-driven limousine pulled up at the door.

"It was an absolute pleasure, Miss Gordon. Tell your grandfather I hope he's feeling more like himself soon, won't you?"

Anne assured him she would, and even promised to see the movie once it reached the theatres.

147

Blaine moved lightly down the front steps and got into the waiting car. It swished out of sight moments later behind the high shrubbery massing the driveway.

Peter James followed the car with his eyes. "Good riddance," he said at last.

"Oh? He seemed very pleasant company." Anne gave him an innocent, wide-eyed stare.

"He was – until Diana developed other interests. And it's not that diver, either!"

So who had Diana been seeing? Anne opened her mouth to ask the question and then closed it again. She felt a cold knot in the pit of her stomach. Could Diana possibly be interested in Alex Stryker? As the thought crossed her mind, Anne attempted to ignore the surge of jealousy that accompanied her suspicion. She hadn't seen Stryker since the night at the Pier House. Perhaps the reason he had never called back concerned Diana Moon!

Peter James frowned, as though realizing that he had been silent an unnaturally long time. He held out his hand.

"I'm afraid I must be running along, too. I promised Aldridge that I would stop in and see him about the script. Some sort of trivial technicality, but necessary none-the-less." Peter James, after staring beyond the veranda to the azure-colored sea beyond, departed.

Anne finally moved to return inside. All of the movie people seemed nice enough; yet she thought back on the number of times that they had been out on the *Riga* for one reason or another. Devlin had a tendency to let everyone wander all over his ship. Anne bit her lip thoughtfully, and wondered if any of the movie company knew how to scuba dive.

The sun radiated white-hot shafts of heat from high in the sky later that day. Anne drove into Key West, watching carefully to see if someone followed her, but spied nobody. She had decided to keep the rendezvous with Leigh and stopped at the bank to cash traveler's checks; one purpose in her remaining at Islamorada was to find the murderer and saboteur. If Leigh had the information, Anne had decided not to quibble about the source, as long as it could be purchased for the right price. And the money had never been a problem; at least her grandfather and Colin wouldn't have to be brought into the transaction.

Afterward, Anne strolled in and out of the different shops after deciding to remain in town. The place had changed in her five years' absence; besides, at this hour of the afternoon not many tourists crowded the streets because of the extreme heat.

She took her time, ambling along, gaping at postcards, knick-knacks, sharks' teeth, and endless numbers of shells; posted on just about every window appeared a recipe for Key Lime Pie. One particularly attractive-looking store specialized in enamel wares. A little farther on she noted a "shell barn", where different types of seashells had been polished for possible sale; Anne saw the conches, of course, plus other types with their lovely shades of lavender, ochre, pink and peach. She wandered up and down the aisles in the store, gazing raptly. Sand dollars, those shells so typical of the Keys and of Florida in general, had been lacquered and hung on chains as souvenirs for tourists.

As Anne leaned over the glass, staring, she saw them. It didn't register for a minute, but blonde hair like hers shone like a spotlight and made it impossible to be completely anonymous. The sunglasses, strangely enough, made her more recognizable, not less, perhaps because as a movie star, she had been photographed so many times and they had become a part of her image.

The man stood next to her, head half-turned away. As Anne saw his familiar blonde, bleached hair, she felt a lurch of something like surprise. As the man moved farther around, Anne dived behind a display of lobster pots while continuing to peer ahead. Cristel Slivka's words from their Cedar Key photography shop played back right here in Key West.

"His latest interest is called Deidre or Debbie someone. I heard about her from the people at the Club. She's in movies, too…"

The name hadn't been Deidre or Debbie, but Diana. Diana Moon.

Fortunately, both parties appeared so engrossed in their conversation that they didn't bother looking up. Diana hadn't been having a secret meeting with Stryker; the actress was seeing Anne's ex-husband Leigh!

Somehow Anne made it down the aisle without anyone noticing; she fled past a sales clerk, receiving a very perplexing look, indeed. Strangely enough, the unintentional voyeurism made Anne feel guilty as she reached the narrow street, careened around a corner of a refreshment stand and stopped to catch her breath.

She finally meandered to the Volkswagen and drove absentmindedly toward Islamorada. A meeting between Leigh and Diana had to be significant – but for what? Could Leigh be the murderer? The thought came and went all in the same second; Leigh had many nasty faults, but killing people wasn't one of them. No, far more likely he had known Diana simply because he appeared on stage himself – or wanted to appear. Knowing Leigh, he likely used the actress as a source of information, pumping her for all she knew. And through Diana, he could keep track of everyone's activities at Gordon Hall, since he'd remained *persona non grata* as long as David Gordon lived.

The sun had set by the time Anne ran the car up the last small rise to the entrance of the estate. The house seemed quiet with an almost drowsy feeling still about it. Ten o'clock and the heat withered everyone who was up and around.

Anne returned to her room and checked the tree house before going to bed. It remained comfortably dark with no flashing lights to mar the ebony blackness of the woods. Strangely, this did not have a calming effect; instead, it made her more nervous. Finally, in an illogical gesture of defiance, she got up and shut the doors to the veranda, leaving Jezebella outside in the cool night air. Despite the suffocating heat, Anne had a feeling that sleep would come much faster. Surprisingly enough, it did.

<<<<*Gordon*>>>>

The following day, Wednesday, Anne came down late to breakfast and found Diana Moon the only other person in the dining room. Diana smiled rather uncertainly as Anne slid into a place opposite her.

She poured some coffee and thought about the last time she'd seen Diana with Leigh. Anne studied her from under lowered lashes; the actress looked decidedly uneasy as she munched on a piece of dry toast. Anne wondered what Leigh had told her, but more importantly, what had the two of them been talking about yesterday in the Shell Shop?

151

The actress appeared as though she wanted to say something, but didn't know how to start. Anne decided to open the conversation with what she hoped was a neutral subject, draw her in, and make life a bit easier for both of them.

"How's the movie coming?" she queried, taking a sip of coffee.

"Not so very well."

Anne recollected that Diana had been more than a little frightened in regard to this particular subject, so she raised her brows in silent interrogation.

"There are these notes and nobody can figure out how they are coming. They just appear, every so often, as though by magic or something."

"I'd like to see all of them. The notes, I mean."

Diana spoke eagerly. "I'm going out to the *Riga* today. Right after I'm done eating. You could come along if you'd like. Actually, I was supposed to go with P.J. and Aldridge earlier, but I overslept, so they seem to have gone without me. But they'll send the boat back, I'm sure."

Anne wondered if the diver who would be taking them to the *Riga* would be Jack Cole. She could understand his willingness for the job if Diana turned out to be his passenger. Spending another day on the water hadn't been part of Anne's plan, but she might glean additional facts from the trip. Opportunity beckoned, so to speak.

"Okay. I would like to come." She might also see Alex Stryker; just the thought of him made her heart thud faster and her eyes brighten.

Diana stirred her coffee with slow deliberate movements, her eyes following the ripples in the dark brown liquid. She glanced up suddenly.

"I saw you yesterday in town. In the Shell Shop when I met Leigh."

Anne's face froze into what she prayed looked like a noncommittal expression.

"Really?" She tried to make her voice sound bland, but failed miserably. Strangely, Diana seemed to understand.

"Don't worry, Anne. I didn't tell him anything. We just happened to meet and started to talk. I knew him in California, you see. When I was first learning to become an actress," she added ingeniously. "I've been spending more time in Key West. It's lonely out here. I mean with P.J. and Aldridge always off looking for location shots. And Frank gone, too. I haven't known what to do with myself. But I didn't say anything to Leigh about you."

Then what did you talk about, Anne wondered. Diana's face looked almost childishly appealing despite the heavy makeup. Perhaps she spoke the truth. Of course, there was no telling what Leigh had managed to get on the side, without the actress even being aware of it. And since David Gordon had made his granddaughter the heir of Islamorada…

"It doesn't matter," Anne said gently. "Leigh and I have been divorced for over a year. He's a free agent."

The other woman seemed relieved.

"I wasn't quite sure. I was wandering around with nothing to do and he came up, exactly like old times."

"Don't worry about it." Anne had heard enough about Leigh Giddings for the morning and besides, the damage had been done. She stood up, anxious to change the subject. "Look, I'd like to take a few more pictures. I'll get my camera and be right down. We can meet in the boathouse. That's where they'll be expecting us to turn up."

As Diana nodded, Anne slid out the door, hurried to her room and got the Nikon. Glancing out the window beyond the veranda, she could see the actress ambling on ahead, taking her time going through the rose garden. Anne scurried downstairs to try and catch up.

Coming across the lawn, Diana stopped and hesitated before going into the boathouse. One of the divers would be there in a few minutes to ferry them out to the *Riga*. Anne looked across the water, half-expecting to see Jack Cole or one of the others on the way to the wharf.

Then Diana began to scream.

She screamed over and over as Anne ran toward the boathouse door and swung it back. The sound rang in her ears as she plowed straight inside and promptly fell over an old anchor. But that didn't claim her attention. On the floor, directly ahead, she saw a man's body, still dressed in the same clothes as the last time she'd seen him. He wouldn't be needing fifty thousand dollars now or ever; someone had bashed in the side of his head – and Leigh was undeniably quite dead.

Chapter Seventeen

*"Is that a DEATH?
And are there two?
Is DEATH that woman's mate?"*
The Rime of the Ancient Mariner
(Samuel Taylor Coleridge)

They gathered in the main room of Gordon Hall in two separate groups – the Gordon family, consisting of Anne, Robin and Maud; and the movie people: Peter James, Aldridge Thornton and Diana Moon, who had made a temporary recovery from her bout of hysterics. The police had arrived, called by Colin after Anne had run back to the house with a screaming Diana in tow. Two police cars had parked by the boathouse along with an ambulance. As they watched the scene below, several people left the wharf area and began walking toward the veranda; although Anne squinted her eyes, she still didn't recognize anyone.

She turned and wandered across the room; Aldridge Thornton offered her a chair which Anne gladly accepted. She wedged herself into a comfortable corner and attempted to remain calm. Then Colin Grant appeared at the door.

"The Lieutenant wants to talk to us individually," he reported to nobody in particular. He stamped almost angrily over to one of the straight-backed chairs; once there, his attitude changed and he slumped wearily.

155

"But that's ridiculous," Peter James broke in. "The police can't suspect that one of us killed the fellow, surely? Why I've never seen the man before in my life!"

Aldridge nodded his head in agreement.

Diana, propped on the sofa with several cushions behind her, didn't bother saying anything at all.

"Miss Gordon is the person they should talk to," P.J. muttered. "The man is her husband."

"Was my husband," Anne retorted acidly. "I haven't been close to Leigh in months."

"But did you know why he was here? I gather he's been sneaking around for a long time."

Anne shot a glance at Diana, wondering if she'd planned to speak up about knowing Leigh. But the woman's eyes remained closed and her lips resolutely still.

"Look," Anne said impatiently. "I'll go first, if it will make you feel better – to see this Lieutenant or whoever – since you seem to think it's so significant that Leigh and I married five years ago."

Colin held up a hand for peace.

"I'm positive Mr. James wasn't accusing anybody of anything. But why don't you go on ahead. They were insistent about talking to you anyway."

She glared at Colin, feeling deserted by everyone. Robin gave her an encouraging smile, but the others studiously avoided her eyes. Anne eased out of her chair and stood up.

"He's in the reception room on the other side of the hall," Colin called, unnecessarily.

Once out of sight of everyone, Anne's initial courage deserted her. Then she shrugged. Why should she be worried; there was no longer a tie between Leigh and

156

herself – it was non-existent. Surely the fact that they had been married couldn't make so much of a difference. Many other people had known him and there had to be at least one of them who wanted him to die.

What had he planned to tell you, the voice inside her head piped up? What had been worth fifty thousand dollars? She didn't know and never would, now that Leigh had died. Anne firmly pushed this thought away, opened the door and walked into the morning room.

The room had always reminded Anne of a closet sort of affair that looked like it had been tacked onto the rest of the house at the last minute. Her gaze traveled from the beige wallpaper and red draperies to the oversized desk near the window. As her eyes focused on the man seated there, she felt her mouth fall open.

"Stryker." Anne's lips moved, but no sound came out. The man wore a conservative three-piece suit and radiated a feeling of police efficiency that had been totally absent before. And as she looked into his cool gray eyes, she realized he was the police lieutenant who had been so insistent about speaking with her.

>>>>*Gordon*>>>>

Stryker noticed Anne Gordon's eyes grow wide in shocked surprise. She blinked rapidly, almost as though she thought her mind deceived her.

Stryker rose smoothly in one fluid motion and eased around the desk; he didn't want to startle her even more. Anne looked like a small Key West miniature deer, caught in the headlights of a car and unable to move.

"You! You're with the police? Why didn't you tell me?"

"Sit down, please!"

He eased her into the chair opposite.

"Try to understand. I couldn't! I wanted to, so many times. But I was under strict orders. And once I was convinced that the divers' deaths were murder…"

"But how can you be so sure?" Anne's gaze focused entirely on Stryker.

"Too many accidents. Accidents don't follow a pattern and these did. Your brother could have been part of the pattern five years ago. I'm just not sure!"

"Edward." Anne licked her lips. "You think he might have been murdered?"

"I don't know!" He watched as her mouth twisted down in a bitter line.

"And my falling for you? Was that part of the pattern, too?" Her voice rose sharply. "To find out what I knew?"

Alex rose and came around the desk. He knelt down next to her.

"I fell for you, too. It's that simple. I love you, Anne. It might have started as something else in the beginning, but I love you. If you don't believe anything else, believe me when I say that!"

He saw her frown lighten. A look of confusion replaced the anger.

"So…"

Stryker returned to the desk chair.

"I'm sorry. But I need to ask you about Leigh. I need to know if you had any idea at all what he would be doing at the boathouse. And what you and Ms. Moon were doing down there yourselves."

Anne drew a deep breath.

"Diana had been invited out to the dive boat. I was going with her, to look around and take more pictures. We

158

walked to the wharf since Mr. Devlin had indicated he would send one of the divers for us in the whaler. And she found Leigh's body while we were waiting."

"So Miss Moon found the body first?"

"Uh-huh. I heard her scream and rushed in."

"And you knew your ex-husband was in the neighborhood?" Stryker gave her a cursory look.

"I'd seen him twice. The first time he wanted money. I gave him some and he left. I thought permanently."

"Why?" he queried quietly, his eyes watching her face.

She studiously looked at the desk, as though she found it the most interesting one in existence.

"I felt sorry for him, I guess. He'd been having a run of bad luck and…"

Stryker rose abruptly and paced to the far side of the little room.

"And you just shelled out to him? Couldn't you see what a leech he was?"

"At least he was up front with me about what he wanted and didn't sneak around behind my back under false pretenses, gathering information about all of us!" Anne's voice rose an octave. "How dare you criticize! I gave him money and he left. At least that's what I thought. Period. So what?"

Stryker's face looked flushed and he ran his fingers through his hair. A long pause followed.

"You said there was another time?" He tried to control his voice.

"Down on the beach. Leigh had information he wanted to sell for fifty thousand dollars. I had to meet him tonight in the boathouse with the money and he said he would come across with something else – something important."

Stryker's eyes betrayed his interest.

"Did he give you any idea what this was?"

"No. Just that it was urgent. Now he's dead, so I suppose we'll never know."

Several minutes went by with neither of them saying a word. The ticking of the ormolu clock on the nearby coffee table sounded abnormally loud. Stryker watched her closely.

Finally he spoke. "You're sure there's nothing else?"

"What else would there be? I have no idea what Leigh was doing in the boathouse at that hour of the morning."

"He wasn't killed there. It appears he was murdered elsewhere and left in the boathouse for someone to find. The body was already cold. He had been killed hours ahead of when you and Diana discovered him."

"But why didn't Aldridge Thornton or Peter James find him? They left for the *Riga* from the wharf earlier."

"Thornton and James didn't go inside. The two went straight to the dive ship. You and Miss Moon seem to have been the next people to approach the building."

"Do you have any idea who the murderer is? You've been out on the *Riga* for weeks!"

"It's not as easy as it sounds. There are a lot of divers coming and going, new hires, second shift, whatever. Nobody seems to have a motive for not wanting to find treasure. The divers all get a percentage of each find. We can't discover any connection between the murders and the people on board. There are so many individuals who have access including some here at

Gordon Hall – plus the incident with Tom Saunders at Water World. He's dead, too."

Anne's eyes reflected her shock as Alex related what had happened to Saunders.

"I liked Tom. He was my friend. And now you say he's gone, too. He worked for my grandfather and knew the waters and currents. But…"

Stryker's sphinx-like eyes showed his extreme interest. "But?"

"I just don't know what to think! Leigh and Tom Saunders. They're both dead!"

Stryker studied her face. "You're sure you have no idea what, if any, information Giddings might have had?"

"Of course not," Anne snapped back. "Would I have been willing to pay Leigh for something I already knew?"

"It just seems to me," and here Stryker began choosing his words with care, "that you've been close at hand when these crimes were committed."

"And so I'm what? Holding out on you? A suspect? A murderess?"

"If I honestly thought that, you'd be down at police headquarters. No, my point is, watch out for yourself. You could be in danger."

Her mouth dropped open in surprise for the second time in the last half-hour.

"You think he may be after me? But why?"

"Why Leigh – or Saunders? Or the divers? We're cautioning everyone to be careful. Don't wander around alone, and certainly not at night. And if you think of anything else…"

"Give you a call," she finished for him. Anne rose and moved away from the desk. "I'll send in the next possible victim. Happy hunting, Alex. I hope you're successful in your search."

Stryker opened and closed his mouth without saying a word as Anne rose, moved to the door and quietly left.

>>>>*Gordon*>>>>

Aldridge Thornton had been delegated to face Stryker after Anne left the morning room. She wasn't sure by what means the group surrounding the fireplace in the main room had determined it. Drawn straws, maybe?

She fended off Robin and Colin who waited near the stairwell; Maud had vanished earlier. Anne escaped to her room, thoroughly disgusted with the world in general. As she passed by the dining room, she saw a uniformed officer by the front door and another outside patrolling the veranda. The police had arrived in force.

The room when she reached it felt stifling hot; Anne dragged herself out onto the veranda. A sharp, cutting breeze blowing in from the sea helped banish the heat.

I should have known, Anne thought morosely. A fantastically attractive man gives me the evening of a lifetime. Yet, I wonder. Does Stryker really love me?

Suspicions and doubts crowded Anne's mind. Then she sighed. Why did there have to be a possible motive behind it all?

The loud voices from the garden below took a while to penetrate her dark, private thoughts. Finally, looking down, she saw the two people below.

Diana Moon and Peter James had been having a heated conversation; loud angry tones carried to the veranda, although Anne couldn't hear every word. Diana's voice seemed lower, placating, but then James turned, his back stiffly arched and marched into Gordon Hall.

Diana watched him before she raised her eyes and saw Anne. She looked taken aback, but finally she waved.

Anne hastily left her room and rushed down the stairs. The door to the morning room had been closed and people sat in the main living area. Anne ignored them and rushed to join Diana on the front lawn. Stryker hadn't said anything about staying inside anyway, so why shouldn't she go out?

Diana had seated herself in one of the white cane chairs in the garden. Anne moved and sat down across from her; they both stared silently at the blood-red flowers.

Diana turned then for the first time, her eyes wide with fright. Leigh's death appeared to have really affected her. Diana must have allowed her emotions full swing and now she paid the price.

She spoke, in her famous, husky Lauren Bacall voice that was known in theatres throughout the world. "I tried to leave, to get away, back to L.A., to escape from the curse and the dead souls. But…" she closed her eyes and whimpered softly, "that Lieutenant wouldn't let me go. I'm stuck here in all this," she waved her arm vaguely toward the rose garden with its overgrown path leading to the glistening white sand beyond, somehow managing to include the entire Islamorada estate, "since he doesn't want anybody leaving the Key West area. And…I don't feel safe here! It was bad enough with those accidents on the boat. That had something to do with the *San Pedro's* treasure. But this maniac is attacking everyone!"

"You have some idea who it is?"

163

"No, but it almost has to be a man. I mean," and here she looked surreptitiously around, "not that many of the women dive – just you and Robin. But I don't think it's either of you," she added hastily. "I think he's crazy. And I've got to get away before I'm next!' Her voice rose to almost a crescendo on the last word.

"I don't agree. About his being crazy, that is. I think there's a pattern to what is happening, a reason. If only someone could see it!"

"Diana," Anne grasped her shoulders and held on hard, forcing the woman to look up. "I need your help. Leigh had some information he was going to sell to me. You were the last person to see him alive. Did he say anything at all, about Islamorada or these mysterious deaths, anything that might help me?"

She frowned as though honestly trying to remember. Then she shook her ash-blonde head. "Nothing about you. Or Islamorada."

"What about where he'd been keeping himself? Where was he staying since he'd come back to Key West?"

"On the beach. And in the tree house. He talked a lot about the tree house. But honestly, he didn't say anything in particular about the murders."

"Try to recollect. It could be important. What about the tree house?"

But she shook her head and shuddered.

"Nothing will happen in daylight," Anne murmured sympathetically. "Just try and get hold of yourself. There are all these people around, plus the police!"

"I don't care! I just want to leave!"

And the actress began rocking back and forth, moaning softly as though the souls of the dead Indians really had cursed the estate and everyone on it. Nothing Anne could say would change her mind.

Chapter Eighteen

"In broken mathematics, We estimate our prize,
Vast, in its fading ratio, to our penurious eyes!"
Part Four: Time and Eternity (Emily Dickinson)

Peter James eventually appeared after his interview with Stryker and led a sobbing, shaking Diana back to her room. As she watched the two of them disappear into Little Isle, Anne realized that she had been presented with a golden opportunity. While everyone was occupied with the police, she could go and take another look at the tree house, since, according to Diana, Leigh had been talking about it shortly before he died. And maybe she could find out exactly what had been so important about the place. It couldn't be hazardous, since the entire group, aside from herself, Diana and P.J. had been summoned inside, talking with Alex Stryker.

She turned sharply from the drive and cut back through the garden. The overly sweet scent of the magnolias reached out to her, enveloping in their odor. Hurrying on, she rushed through the woods pushing rapidly into the undergrowth. As she glanced down, she saw the footprints, leading directly toward the tree house; these had been Leigh's tracks. A swarm of egrets burst from the bushes ahead and shot skyward, flapping their wings in alarm, but she ignored them as the goal came into sight.

Anne didn't even stop to catch her breath, but scurried up the ladder. Once at the top, she pulled herself onto the solid wood and vanished through the doorway.

She peered around the room, much as she had the last time. The couch along one wall appeared deeply indented as though someone had slept there. Leigh had been here last night, perhaps sleeping, right before he died. She turned slowly, searching carefully. What in the simply furnished place could be important enough to die for?

She began running her hands across the well-worn furniture, starting with the couch, checking for a hiding place of sorts. There had to be something somewhere! When nothing came to light, Anne looked at the wooden planking comprising the floor. In all the mysteries she had seen on television, the treasure or whatever was hidden in a secret compartment in the floor; although Anne rapped and stared at each crevice in her best Nancy Drew manner, she found absolutely zero.

She stopped and sat back on her heels to think of where else to try. Perhaps Alex Stryker should be told about this latest clue, yet Anne didn't want to give up the search – at least, not yet.

Her gaze traveled past the table and couch to the storage cabinet where the food had been kept. It had been a good hiding place for the games she and Edward played long ago. Anne sat back and closed her eyes tight. If she could just remember…

Suddenly, she was ten years old again, hauling herself up the tree house ladder. *One step at a time. Hand over hand. Please don't let me fall! And don't look down! She'd almost reached her goal; Edward's face peered over at her, the late afternoon sun glinting off his hair, turning it into a reddish-blonde burnished flame.*

"Hurry up, Annie! I have a surprise! I pinched something from our toady friend, Colin Grant!"

Anne pulled herself up the last few steps and collapsed on the porch, exhausted. Her eyes were drawn past the ladder of the tree house to the ground. Such a long way down! A wave of dizziness overwhelmed her.

"Don't look down, stupid! You'll get sick for sure. And then you won't get to try this!"

He held up the package of cigarettes triumphantly toward her. "Go ahead. Take one. I've always wanted to try."

"Edward! We shouldn't! Grandfather will have a fit. And suppose Mr. Grant finds out you swiped his cigarettes?"

"Grandfather will never know – unless you tell!" Edward pulled some matches from the pocket of his jeans. The name tag bracelet he always wore glinted like spun gold in the half-light. He scratched one match, lit the cigarette, and passed it to her.

"That's it. Watch me!"

Edward lit another cigarette and drew the smoke deep into his lungs. He coughed harshly.

Anne giggled. She blew the smoke out into an imaginary ring right before she started choking. Edward pounded her on the back.

"Edward, I don't feel so good. And..."

"Wait! What's that?" He held up a hand that commanded silence. In the distance, a woman's voice could be heard.

Anne looked nervously around. "It's Aunt Maud! What are we going to do?"

"Do?" Edward rose and stepped hard on the cigarette. "Why, we'll hide these and come back later! Here, look at this. Stop choking and come on! I have something else to show you!"

He moved to the cupboard inside the tree house and yanked it open. Anne peered inside.

"What is it? What's there?"

"This!" and magically a dark hollow cavern appeared inside the back of the cupboard. Edward dropped the cigarettes and matches inside and...

Anne jackknifed to her feet and pulled open the heavy oak door as Edward had done so long ago. A few cans of food, matches, and a flashlight remained on the shelves. Anne shoved it all aside and stared closely at the back panel of the cupboard. It had to be here somewhere! She began rapping on the wood, starting at the far right hand corner and moving downward.

Anne had almost reached the bottom when she noted one section of panel sounded distinctly hollow. She rapped again, kneeling over the area. Yes, she'd found it! Her fingers probed at the wood, searching for a lever to open the door; finally, she accidently touched the lower right hand corner section, revealing a dark hole, approximately a foot square. Anne crammed her head into the opening in her eagerness before leaning back in disgust.

"It's empty! Completely unquestionably empty!" she muttered aloud. Someone had beaten her to the loot or money or whatever. It was gone now, gone just like Leigh.

Anne got up and dusted off her clothes. The tree house seemed to have been used as a hiding place, but she had no idea for what or by whom.

Anne crawled down the ladder and began the long trudge to the house. The hope of finding something, anything that would tell her who had caused the wave of terror surrounding Gordon Hall died. All she had done was to discover another false trail!

The daylight had almost vanished; the sun cast long, golden shadows on the aquamarine sea. She noted that the police cars had disappeared from in front of the house, but had been transferred to the wharf. Stryker must have decided to return and examine the boathouse for additional evidence.

Colin Grant confirmed this as Anne wearily slipped past him and sat down on the sofa in the main room. The group had dispersed; everything seemed still. Colin sat opposite, his legs stretched out, entirely exhausted.

"Did Alex say anything to you, Colin? About who the police think is responsible?"

"Not a word. Just asked questions and more questions! Stryker and that assistant of his that turned up – Catalano or some name like it."

"They must know something by now!"

"Stryker said he was going to talk to Devlin again on the *Riga.* Maybe we'll have peace for a while."

"What about my grandfather? He wasn't disturbed, I hope?"

"No. But he'll want to hear all the whys and wherefores. Not that I have all that many whys and wherefores to tell." Colin pushed himself reluctantly to his feet. "I think that your grandfather is about the only person here that the Lieutenant doesn't suspect. He can't have committed the murders, since he can't get out of bed!"

"Go ahead, Colin. I know my grandfather will want to hear everything. And tell him," as he paused in the doorway, "tell him I'll be along later – before dinner."

"Right." He waved and disappeared. Anne leaned back in her chair and tried to relax, but she couldn't let go of the events of the afternoon, searching for the key that would uncover the answer to the whole riddle because there had to be a motive. At least, Anne hoped so; if a mass murderer had gone on a killing spree, they were in far more trouble than she would have ever believed possible.

>>>>*Gordon*<<<<

Shadows announced the descent into evening of the same day. Anne watched from the veranda while Stryker and two other men disembarked from the police launch after it docked. She studied their faces, but they told her nothing. She saw Alex pause and look toward the main house, but then he turned and followed the other officers. Shortly after, the police departed.

Anne entered Islamorada and shut the door with a bang; the place remained quiet with no sound at all. She hesitated and decided to visit her grandfather.

Surprisingly, she found him completely alone. For once, Maud seemed to be absent, rather than lurking around the corners. David Gordon's blue eyes opened suddenly and he peered up.

"Anne." She caught the trace of the smile which crossed his lips. He attempted to move, but his face became contorted in a grimace.

"Are you in pain? Is there anything I can do?"

"Do? Nothing anybody can do at this point. Blasted doctors. Don't know their right hand from their left half the time. All they're good for is spouting off twenty-five

171

letter words at the mouth! If they help a person stay alive, it's an accident! And if they cure someone, it's a miracle! Nothing more!"

Anne could feel herself begin to relax at his speech; David Gordon sounded more like his usual irascible self. She sat down in an antique-satin chair, probably as priceless as it was uncomfortable. She folded her hands in her lap and waited.

Her grandfather seemed curious about everything that had been happening. His questions came fast and furious.

After relating the events of the day, Anne paused for breath. David Gordon spoke quietly.

"Did this Lieutenant…Stryker you said his name is, give you any idea about who could be the guilty party?"

"No, not a word. But Colin told you all about that."

"I haven't seen Colin all day. Some business manager I've got!"

"Perhaps I misunderstood what he said." Anne spoke soothingly, but her mind absorbed this new information. She'd thought that Colin would be coming straight upstairs. If he hadn't come here, then where could he have gone?

"Anne, do me a favor. Be especially cautious. I have a very bad feeling about this whole business. First the accidents on the *Riga*. Then Saunders. And now it's your ex-husband. Granted, I never had much use for the fellow, but I didn't particularly want to see him die."

"You think that someone might be interested in hurting me? But why?"

"I don't know. That's the worst part of the whole thing. I don't know why any of the murders have occurred. Why should anyone harm the divers or try and hinder the search for the *San Pedro* and the treasure? Everyone will gain from what is found. At least as far as I know."

"Don't worry. I plan to be careful. I want to be alive when they catch this maniac. And that is exactly what I'm beginning to think he is!"

"If he's crazy, it's a clever kind of crazy." The old man said dryly. "He's killed four people. Even with this Lieutenant posing as a diver, the murderer managed to commit a crime right under Stryker's nose. The police should be half as bright. They would have caught the fellow ten times over!"

Anne leaned across and kissed his forehead.

"I'll take care. Actually, I thought for a while that Alex might be involved. And he turns out to be the only safe person in the bunch!"

Her grandfather studied her under half-closed lids. "I guess that depends on what you mean by safe."

She rose and turned to leave. "Would you like me to start your cassette machine?"

"No!" he snarled, suddenly irascible. "I don't want to hear any more 'best of times, worst of times' talk. Don't know why these *Recording for the Blind* people can't do *"Playboy"* or some such." He paused for breath. "And send in Robin. I want to be sure that she's aware of the danger!"

"After having the police traipsing all over Islamorada for the entire afternoon, I should think she would be," Anne muttered. "Okay. I'll send her along."

As she moved to the door, she noted that her grandfather's eyes had closed and he looked so peaceful. Anne walked out into the hall and down to Robin's room. Glancing in, she saw the unmade bed, ransacked closet,

173

and clothes strewn on the floor. Robin had gone. And she had definitely left Gordon Hall in a very great hurry.

For no reason, Anne felt uneasy; something had to happen and soon. She hurried into her own bedroom and saw the white slip of paper propped on the night table.

As she tore open the envelope, Anne's hands started shaking nervously. The note confirmed her apprehensions.

"Dear Anne," Robin began.

"Jack and I are going to be married. Please don't follow and please break the news to my grandfather as gently as possible. I'm in love with Jack and convinced that this is for the best."

Robin

Anne stared at the paper with the two words "please" repeatedly underlined. Feeling as though she'd been moving in slow motion, Anne snatched her purse and ran from the room. They would go straight to Miami; it would be the easiest place for Robin to get lost in the crowd. Too many people in Key West knew the Gordons; the pair had to go inland to the east coast.

As Anne stumbled from Gordon Hall, the heavy wooden door slammed sharply behind her. The car had remained parked by the garage where it had been left earlier in the day. She glanced at the sky; the blue hazy mist of the evening had changed to deep amber, heralding the arrival of night. In a matter of minutes it would be dark, which would complicate the search.

Anne slid behind the wheel. She turned the Volkswagen around and shifted into drive; the car bounded ahead, almost of its own volition, down the road and out of the gates. Anne only hoped that she had found the note in time to catch them.

Chapter Nineteen

"I will put enmity between you and the woman.*"*
            The Holy Bible, Genesis:
            The Lord God to the Serpent.

Anne slammed her foot onto the accelerator as the car dove wildly past the first corner on the way to Route One. Her mind focused on Robin, who seemed determined to make the exact mistake she had made five years earlier. Why hadn't their grandfather been more patient with her? What had pushed her into this running-away act?

As the wheels spun, Anne caught the scent of hot, burning rubber. Looking ahead, she glimpsed the velvet-black sea and the beach beyond. Take it easy, she cautioned. Getting killed wouldn't help Robin in the least. The car churned on gravel as she slowed slightly. The road twisted and turned, the Volkswagen's headlights cutting a swath of white through the darkness. Then everything went black again.

Anne pushed her hair back absentmindedly from her forehead; the car felt stifling hot. She opened the window wide on the driver's side and reached for the radio, hoping the music might help her to relax.

As she leaned over, fingers outstretched, her hand brushed something cold and slippery. Anne felt her body stiffen as she heard the warning rattle. A poisonous reptile had crawled into her car! Her breath caught half-way down her throat; dragging her eyes from the road, she could barely see the snake, half-on, half-off the seat. As the road turned sharply right, she took the curve on two wheels.

Anne risked another cautious glance downward; the snake had slithered a few inches farther away, but suddenly, it serpentined back. The head appeared grossly overgrown with the poison glands embedded in its neck. Another curve came up; this one banked left. The snake moved within striking distance and the warning rattle buzzed harshly.

The rattler uncoiled itself and Anne felt a moment of sheer panic. Her body pressed tight against the side of the car, as far away from the snake as possible. Two more curves came and went; normally they seemed mild, but the car careened down the road at over ninety miles an hour. Now the snake reached three-quarters of the way across the seat. It stopped and coiled its scaly body; Anne had the urge to be suddenly sick.

Her eyes moved once more to the snake away from the road as the car spun from the far left back to the right lane. Suddenly, two blazing headlights illuminated the Volkswagen; the driver of the oncoming car approached much too fast.

Anne yanked at the wheel frantically and her car hurled right, missing the other vehicle by about half an inch. An angry face peered out as the Volkswagen shot past. The snake appeared very close now; looking down, Anne could see the forked tongue flickering in and out. She jerked the wheel left as the snake struck.

It hit the wheel where her hand had been. As the reptile fell back, Anne glanced toward the windshield. The car had left the road.

She tramped on the brakes as the little Volkswagen spun over the rocks. The snake fell against the off-side door as the automobile hit the water and started to sink. Anne knew the place where the car had left the road; she had a number of seconds before it would be filled with water.

Anne slipped off her shoes, keeping one cautious eye on the rattler before yanking on the door. The water streamed inside; she pulled free of the car, fighting for control against the shock of the sea.

Anne kicked upward and a few moments later, hit the surface. She could see the shoreline in the distance, started to swim and prayed silently for the strength to reach it. As Anne touched the rocks, she glanced back. The car had vanished beneath the waves; she had been lucky leaving the road at this point since a solid stone wall retainer stood five hundred feet farther on.

When Anne could finally move, she sat up slowly. Tremors ran through her whole body. Anne pulled herself erect on legs that were wobbly and staggered inland toward the road that led to Islamorada, stopping often to rest on the way back.

How had the rattler gotten into the car? The reptiles had adapted themselves to swimming in the sea, but they had always been found throughout Florida; the Everglades were packed full of them. Could the snake have crawled in accidently? Logic said no. Someone had deliberately put it inside and set her up with a note from Robin; that note likely as false as everything else that had happened. Whoever had done this knew of her attachment to her cousin and had reasoned that, given a motive, Anne could be maneuvered into using the automobile. Once inside, she would either be fatally bitten, or have an accident by driving off of the road. But who had been responsible? Who could have set the trap that had almost ended her life, and more important, for what purpose? Stryker had warned her about wandering around; given these particular circumstances, her actions had been so grossly predictable that they seemed almost comic.

Someone had tried to commit murder, trying for an accident similar to the divers out on the *Riga*. It would seem to be the same type of coincidence. In reality, the attempt on her life appeared as one in a long series of events that had occurred at Islamorada.

Anne began walking to Gordon Hall on legs that had finally stopped quivering. She decided to tell her grandfather and the others that the car had skidded and gone off the road; Colin could send someone to salvage the Volkswagen. Meanwhile, Anne needed to watch them all, very carefully, as she made an entrance. Perhaps someone, seeing her back from the dead so to speak, might make a mistake.

Had Robin and Jack Cole actually eloped? If so, they had far too great a head start to stop them. Anne felt indescribably weary as she walked toward home.

>>>>*Gordon*<<<<

It didn't take long before the heavy iron gates marking the entrance to Gordon Hall came into view; Anne marched inside and proceeded to the house. But something appeared wrong; the Hall had been lit up like a Christmas tree. She ran up the front veranda, yanked open the heavy oak door, and hurried into the room beyond.

A highly distracted Robin ran into the room. As Anne looked up the stairs, she saw Maud standing firmly like a black specter by the banister.

179

"Where have you been?" Robin stammered finally. "We hunted and hunted! Grandfather Gordon..."

"But your note! I thought you'd gone to Miami!"

That stopped her. Anne had never seen anyone look quite so blank.

"What note?"

Anne wearily shook her head and didn't answer. She had obviously been manipulated by a master of the art.

"I'd been out with Colin and that Lieutenant Stryker on the dive boat most of the day. And when we returned, Grandfather Gordon was much worse!"

Anne looked around the room; everyone had put in an appearance: Colin, Aldridge, Peter James and Maud. They avoided her gaze.

Anne slowly detached herself from Robin and went upstairs to David Gordon's room. The old man lay on the bed, but no labored breathing sounded, no sharp eyes watched her cross the room. The man in the bed would not move again.

Anne stood there for long seconds, staring at him. He seemed smaller and almost withered; hardly the man who had run the Gordon Empire for a quarter of a century. She sat in the chair by his bed and took the hand lying on the spread. Her eyes searched his face; it didn't look peaceful. All the novels spoke of people dying quietly in their sleep, but David Gordon looked as though he had been fighting and in pain, his face contorted even now in a grimace. Anne closed her eyes and could almost hear his voice booming out as it had so often in the past. She carefully tucked his hand inside the sheet before going back downstairs.

Once there, everyone seemed to be wandering from place to place with nowhere in particular to go. Robin talked to Maud, asking about her grandfather's pills. They both moved to meet Anne as she stepped into the main room.

Maud looked tired; dark circles ringed her protruding eyes and her fingers trembled slightly. Nursing David Gordon must have been an exhausting job for her under any circumstance. She dragged her leg awkwardly as though lifting it up had become too much of an effort for the moment.

Maud spoke up. "I took the liberty of calling Ben Caldwell. He said he would be out first thing tomorrow."

Anne nodded. "What about the funeral services? Did my grandfather mention to you where he wanted to be buried?"

"Yes. In the family plot with Laurette and Robin's parents. At Islamorada, of course. He and his wife will finally be together on the estate they both loved."

Her voice did not sound normal and she studiously avoided looking at anyone. She really must have been fond of her brother.

Robin spoke up.

"I was asking Aunt Maud about Grandfather's pills. We can't find them anywhere."

"I told you before, Robin. I had them the last time I went in to see your grandfather. They're temporarily misplaced on a shelf in the bathroom or some such."

Robin still looked unconvinced, but subsided into stillness. Anne thought of her own recent experience with the snake, alongside of the mysterious note that had been planted to get her out of Gordon Hall. Now she knew why.

Anne sat down on the window seat and watched each person in the room. One of them had been responsible for her grandfather's death; one of these people, perhaps more than one, had helped an old man to the grave. Someone had been so impatient, they couldn't wait longer. Coincidence had struck a few too many times for there to be any other answer.

Anne realized that Colin should be told about the car, but it no longer seemed important. Her grandfather's troubleshooter would take care of it as he took care of everything else at Islamorada. Capable, competent, Colin. Anne studied him as he went from one person to another, consoling, comforting, speaking quietly and personally to each individual. Robin had said she and Colin spent the day together. They had returned home shortly before her grandfather's last attack. Anne wondered exactly how long the two had been on the premises before David Gordon's death occurred.

She suspected Colin Grant, David Gordon's most trusted, closest associate, who had been in business with him for years – Colin Grant, who had been a permanent fixture at Gordon Hall. Someone she admired and respected. Yet Anne decided to speak with Robin again; she needed to discover when Colin had come back to the house.

Her grandfather had been lying upstairs, alone and helpless. Anne felt a flicker of anger begin to burn deep inside. No longer would she wait for this person to spring his filthy little traps. No longer would she wait timidly inside of Gordon Hall for the police to catch whoever had been responsible. David Gordon's death must be avenged. He had been a Gordon. And so was she. There was no question about it.

>>>>*Gordon*<<<<

They sat together in the family pew two days later while the minister intoned the last rites over David Gordon's casket in the chapel at Islamorada. Her grandfather had indicated that he wanted a brief service; Colin had been glad to oblige. When the organ resounded loudly throughout the church, Anne rose with the other mourners; the funeral procession moved down the aisle past the elaborate, stained glass windows and outside to the waiting hearse. Maud, Robin and Anne followed closely behind while Colin brought up the rear as they walked behind the casket to the small family cemetery on the estate.

As Anne helped Maud, who limped along heavily on her bad leg, the younger woman glanced around. The movie company stood there, including P.J., Aldridge and Diana, along with Roger Devlin and one of the other divers. Alex Stryker plus another man who could have only been with the police department hovered off to one side. Many of David Gordon's closest acquaintances walked somberly behind them to the gravesite.

It seemed but a short time before the casket was lowered into the ground. David Gordon's wife had been buried to one side of him, while Edward's empty grave stood on the other. Robin remained quiet and still as she had been throughout the entire service with Maud next to her, stark and straight, in her black dress. Ben Caldwell moved to Robin's side; the police kept discreetly back.

As the minister finished his final homily, the mourners shuffled silently back to Gordon Hall. Refreshments had been set out in the main room by the ever thoughtful Tisha. Anne, Maud, Robin and Colin in their stark black circulated among the mourners, trying to appear as welcoming and normal as possible under the circumstances. Considering that her grandfather had been the fifth person to die under mysterious circumstances and that the police guarded every doorway, Anne thought that the family pulled together reasonably well. And, as far as what would come later? She just didn't know.

>>>>*Gordon*<<<<

Afterward, Anne stood silently next to her aunt and cousin, her eyes flooded with tears. If she had been here, perhaps it wouldn't have happened. But she had been lured away by Robin's false note and now her grandfather had died.

Anne hesitated, then slipped away to the breakfast room for just a moment and ran straight into Alex, who obviously had followed her.

"Anne, I had to talk to you. Perhaps now isn't the time but Grant told me about the snake in your car and your grandfather's pills. And you looked so…forsaken? I'm so sorry about what happened."

"One thing Colin didn't tell you. I think somebody deliberately tried to get me out of the way so that they could kill my grandfather. It's all been too convenient." At this point, she spoke more to herself than to him. "His death is my fault."

"You shouldn't feel that way," he said emphatically. "Whoever is responsible would only have devised another plan to accomplish his aims."

"But my grandfather has been so helpless. What could he have done if someone just smothered him with the pillow or…"

"I don't think so. You see, there are the pills the doctor prescribed. It looks like someone may have taken them and substituted aspirin or another similar drug. Not

184

poison that would appear in an autopsy – just something harmless. By not getting those pills the murderer could have hastened your grandfather' death. It's sort of similar to the villain leaving a window wide open so the victim gets pneumonia and dies."

"But where are those pills?"

"Nobody seems to have any idea." Stryker stated succinctly. "And we have conducted an extensive search, believe me. They are probably in the bottom of the sea by now."

Anne mulled this over.

"Alex, what are we going to do?" Anne felt shafts of fear shoot through her. "He's crazy, you know. There's no motive. I've finally become convinced of it." She turned slowly away.

"I don't think so." He paused, as though fumbling for the right words.

Anne turned back toward Stryker. Suddenly it seemed the most natural thing in the world for him to open his arms and for her to walk into them. As his lips came down on hers, Anne forgot the problems and her grandfather's death along with everything else. When she could speak again, she looked deep into his grey-green eyes. His arms tightened around her.

"I haven't been able to think of anything but you since that first meeting in the woods." He smiled suddenly, his finger tracing a line down her cheek. "You'll never know how hard it's been, trying to conduct a murder investigation, when all I've wanted to do is hold you."

"I know. I feel the same way. And I'm so afraid for both of us – but especially for you. You've got to catch the murderer before the maniac kills anyone else. I don't want to lose you, too. I can't lose you, too." She rested her head lightly on his shoulder.

"Anne, I've an idea. But it wouldn't be fair to you if I should be wrong. It's just so fantastic I can hardly believe it myself. We're checking for more facts and there are reports coming in later tonight at headquarters. I think they'll tell us positively one way or the other. There is a motive, Anne. A very obscure motive, but it is present none-the-less. So I want you to promise to be careful. Stay close to the house and away from the sea. Promise me that now like a good girl, so I don't have to worry about you."

"All right. I promise. But can't you give me a hint?" It suddenly seemed imperative to her to know which one of the people who had sat at their table and eaten their food had in reality been plotting to murder her grandfather.

"As soon as I'm sure," he said quietly. 'It's so preposterous, I'd never forgive myself if I made a mistake."

Anne smiled sadly as there was a knock on the door. Stryker's attention turned to Tisha as her homely face appeared around the corner. Already their little interlude was over; Stryker had returned to thinking about his job. Perhaps all policemen acted like this, otherwise they wouldn't be policemen.

"Oops, sorry, Miss Anne. But Mr. Caldwell and some of the others would like to say goodbye to you before they leave." Her eyes traveled silently to Anne and then to Stryker and back again before she turned away.

As her footsteps retreated, Anne turned to Alex as he continued speaking.

"You should be safe tonight. I'm leaving some men outside. By tomorrow, we will be ready to make an arrest. At least, I honestly think so." He pulled her gently to him. "Don't look so worried. It will be all right. I promise. I'm going to make things right again. For you." He ran his fingers slowly over her hair. "For us."

Anne wound her arms around his neck and raised her mouth for his kiss. Her voice was muffled. "Get him this time, Alex, please. I need to feel safe again. Stop this nightmare for all of us. I…" she broke off abruptly.

He smiled then, a cold bitterly hard smile. "Don't worry. I will." His eyes were those of the hunter, going after the hunted, in this case a murderer.

She eased slowly away and left the room. Crossing through the main hall, Anne joined Robin and Maud by the entranceway. Stryker seemed to have vanished behind her, as she bid one person after another goodbye.

Peter James and Aldridge Thornton were the first to leave, followed by Devlin and the others. Ben Caldwell lingered, his eyes following Robin as she bid farewell to the guests. Afterward, the girl slipped silently out of the side door.

Maud moved over to Anne's side.

"It's that Jack Cole fellow. She's going to meet him. And now that my brother is gone…"

"You think there's nothing standing in his way? Is that it?"

Maud nodded silently.

"The will is set. My grandfather isn't here to change anything anymore. I'll see Robin later and talk to her. Try and make her understand that Jack Cole is a fortune hunter and after her money. Just like…"

"Maybe you can convince her not to make the same mistake."

"Maybe my whole ghastly experience with Leigh will have given me some special insight so that I know what to say to Robin. At any rate, I promise to try when she comes back later. After dinner."

Chapter Twenty

"In her sepulcher there by the sea—
In her tomb by the sounding sea."
Annabel Lee (Edgar Allan Poe)

Robin joined everyone for an especially early dinner later that same day, minus Jack Cole. Anne felt relieved, but, regardless, the small group around the dining table seemed subdued to say the least.

Maud sat to Anne's left, making her usual attempts at perfunctory conversation. Anne tried to contribute a share, but her mind roamed elsewhere to Alex Stryker.

What evidence might he be sifting through to find the answer to the riddle that haunted Islamorada? It seemed as though dinner dragged on forever; yet afterward, when Anne fled to her room, she became restless.

Anne slipped downstairs and crept softly over the well-carpeted floor to the outside door. A board creaked somewhere; her head snapped around, searching the semi-darkness. The late afternoon appeared very still. Anne heard her own breathing, which sounded like a wheeze. All remained silent. Finally she slid carefully through the main entranceway and down the veranda steps as the door swung silently shut.

The air had rapidly cooled off outside – too rapidly. Anne felt the fresh breeze whipping through her shirt as the rain moved in. The summer had been dry, but autumn

189

approached and the hurricane season would be starting with a vengeance.

Everything reflected silence outside, especially the house and the boathouse on the wharf. Even Little Isle seemed drenched in darkness. Anne wandered toward the beach, turning over the mystery of Leigh's death followed by Tom Saunders' and her grandfather's. Why had these three people died?   Anne felt deep inside that the murderer picked his victims methodically, according to a plan. The trick seemed to be to discover the plan.

Only one thing remained to be done; to return to the place where she had met Leigh that last morning. Her actual presence might bring back an additional thought or phrase which could help Alex by giving him just one more clue to work with. Granted that Anne had already gone over every word, even every inflection, but perhaps something additional could be learned; at least she needed to try.

The beach looked completely different in the afternoon sunlight, a long, silvery ribbon of sand that serpentined, snakelike, up the coast. The pebbles which had been washed up shimmered as precious stones, while the shells gleamed like small, white fingered hands. Anne kicked off her shoes and waded into the water; she felt tired, drained and unable to think clearly. Her resolve evaporated as fast as the frothy waves washing the sand off the pebbly beach. It seemed a relief to be out of Gordon Hall, if only for this short while.

Anne turned to look at Islamorada. The big house shone weirdly as the sunlight reflected on the Spanish-tiled roof. The air seemed cooler with a stiff breeze blowing off the water; there would be a storm in the not-too-distant future and a very bad one at that.

Anne walked along, kicking up the surf with her bare feet. All too soon, she stood at the place where Leigh had met her, where he had demanded fifty thousand dollars for information he considered extremely important. Had Leigh guessed he might die and would it have made a difference? Likely not. Leigh's mind had been made up; he would not have altered his course no matter what the consequences, to himself or to others.

Anne reached the tall, reedy grasses and directed her gaze along the wide expanse of sand. She had not been down this beach since her return to Islamorada and for a good reason. Five years ago, Edward had died here, trapped beneath a pile of rock while he slowly strangled to death. Anne saw the stones by the dive site; they rose, skyward, reminding her at this distance of a malformed, malignant cone. The land farther along was where she had been rescued by Tom Saunders and where Edward had never resurfaced.

Anne had avoided the area since coming home, but she didn't want to do so now. Moving toward the sea and tramping into the shallow water where the tide went out, she walked onward, one foot after another. Finally she stood at the fatal spot; here Edward had died. And strangely, other things started to focus as well, as if this journey had jarred her memory concerning something that had remained buried for a long time. She again saw the tunnel that Edward had entered. It had to be near, not far off the shore at all. It felt strange that things appeared so different from this angle; a psychiatrist would have said she had tried to block the horror of that day out of her mind forever for her own self preservation. Regardless, Anne knew that it was time she remembered everything.

Anne reached the rocks and then the feeling came waffling back. Someone watched her as at Water World. Twisting around, she hoped to catch a glimpse of the person, but everything remained silent and still, almost mocking in its deadness. Nothing stirred, not even the sea birds, but she couldn't rid herself of the feeling that someone's eyes bore into her from close by.

The wind rushed through the mangrove and cypress trees not far off the water; the restless branches moved continuously. Anne looked again, searching, but saw nothing.

She settled herself on an outcropping of rock, a promontory that hung over the sea. The water rippling below claimed her attention; the silvery sheen seemed mesmerizing, like light falling through a prism glass. Anne felt it calling, pulling her toward the ocean. She paused, then crawled from the rock and into the shallows. The water felt warm; right here, it didn't come up to her knees. Many areas were like this along the Keys and remained so for a long way out, especially at low tide.

Anne looked, curious, at the rocks more closely. The fading sun helped a little, but its light diffused and didn't do that much good. She should have brought a flashlight. There didn't seem to be much to find, but she kept searching, none-the-less, trying to justify coming here in the early evening.

Just like that, Anne saw it, saw the marks on one of the stones. She knelt in the water and examined them; it seemed certain that someone had dragged a boat up this way and had repeatedly tied it here. Someone had used the inlet to get on and off the estate rather than docking at the wharf.

Finally, a real lead! She thought of only one reason for someone to dock here rather than at the boathouse by Gordon Hall. He was doing something that David Gordon wouldn't approve of; something that in all probability was illegal.

What had been brought here? Anne thought of the place in the tree house where Edward had hidden the cigarettes; the two seemed to be connected. The "it" had to be taken and stashed somewhere until a safe moment arrived, safe for retrieval by a person from Gordon Hall. And why not the tree house? The more Anne considered the idea, the more sense the whole thing made. She could hardly wait to tell Stryker about the concrete evidence she had found concerning the crimes that had been occurring at Islamorada.

Anne turned to leave. The wind blew furiously, kicking up little spirals and swirls of foam on the sand and sea. Her slacks had gotten soaked, but she had so many other problems to consider that her clothes remained at the bottom of the list.

Anne stepped forward and froze into immobility as her legs brushed against something. The shadowy depths played tricks; she stared into the water, but everything remained deathly still. Then something caught hold of her ankles and pulled violently. Anne screamed and toppled into the water; an unseen force dragged her relentlessly downward, away from the inlet. She struggled madly, attempting to break loose, screaming silently as something towed her into the depths. Her mouth and eyes filled with water as she completely submerged; still the weight on her ankles pulled downward.

Anne lashed out with her legs and felt the hold break, just for a second. Then it returned, more firmly than ever, and more relentless.

Anne began to strangle as the breath shot out of her lungs; her body demanded air as she began choking and swallowing water. Her ears popped from the depth of the water pressure as someone dragged her steadily out to sea. Finally, she lost consciousness.

>>>>*Gordon*<<<<

Stryker's cell phone buzzed immediately as he entered his Key West apartment. Yanking it out of his pocket, he glanced down.

"Armando. What's your news? I've been waiting to hear from you."

Catalano's voice almost shook in his anxiety to speak. "We've hit pay dirt when checking past history about the Gordons! And I think this could really be important!"

Stryker dropped into a chair, his brows furrowed in concentration.

"So what's the story? Did David Gordon cheat someone out of multimillions of dollars? Or did that troubleshooter of his, Colin Grant, hang someone out to dry for his boss?"

"It's not the old man at all – or Grant. It's..." Catalano paused to gulp in some air, "his sister, Maud – the one who's taken care of him for the last twenty-five years. She's got a secret like you wouldn't believe!"

"Do tell. I'm waiting." Stryker's voice sounded like a ghostly whisper.

"It seems Maud went to a medical clinic in Lausanne, Switzerland. Supposed to have been admitted

194

for anorexia. But…one of our agents tracked down a nurse that took care of her. And the woman was…" Catalano's voice dripped with excitement, "an O.B. nurse. Maud Gordon had a child."

There was no sound from the other end of the line. Alex's mind reeled with the information.

"So who was the father of the boy?"

"Not listed. But…the child wasn't a boy. It was a girl!"

"And…"

"Maud Gordon took the baby back. The old man, her brother, put the girl up for adoption."

"Have you been able to trace the baby's location? Where has this child been for the last twenty-five years?"

"We're checking. It's hard – both the old man and his sister spent a small fortune hushing things up, paying people off and getting the records altered. Plus, there were no computers back then."

"Keep working," Stryker ordered, his voice hard. "If that child survived, she would be directly related to Anne Gordon and her twin brother, Edward, who died five years ago. She might also be more than a little interested in revenge. On top of being a possible heir to Islamorada and the Gordon fortune…"

"The woman would have an excellent motive for trying to eliminate Anne."

"Call me as soon as you get any more information. I'm driving straight over to the estate now. Anne…" Stryker halted as he sought to control his voice, "Anne could be in deadly danger. And she might need all the help that she can get!"

He moved toward the door the second after the cell 'phone deadened. Maybe…just maybe, he might still be in time.

Otherwise, Stryker's eyes narrowed. If the murderess had killed Anne…he would personally hunt the woman down and make her life so hot that the underworld would seem cold by comparison!

>>>>*Gordon*<<<<

The first sensation that Anne felt was cold – freezing bone-chilling cold. She shivered violently and slowly opened her eyes, afraid of what she might see.

A solid rock ceiling on all sides met her gaze; it looked like some sort of cave. The air smelled rank and still as though it hadn't been disturbed for a long time. The place hovered in semi-darkness; over in one corner, an oil lamp provided a small amount of light.

Anne got up stiffly from the patched flannel blanket on which she had been lying; her damp shirt and slacks clung, making her even more uncomfortable. Glancing around, she spotted the small boxes, two of them, close to the mouth of the cave, but they had been encased in metal and couldn't be opened.

She leaned back against the damp wall and shut her eyes, trying to control the feeling of horror that threatened her. When she opened them again, Anne stared at the ceiling for something better to do. Originally the rock had looked solid, but now she spotted the chinks and the pinnacles as the cave rose into the air. Ironically, it looked like a church with the light from the oil lamp casting shadows on the wall as the flame moved back and forth. A church like the chapel where a minister had intoned the last rites over her grandfather, but here, Anne felt nothing holy; this place could possibly be her tomb.

Anne shook her head, trying to banish these morbid thoughts and went back to staring at the light from the oil lamp. She watched it, mesmerized; as a child, she had been fascinated with fire and the fascination had remained.

Anne stared hard at the lamp. Had the light dimmed for a moment? Yes, the flame cast a bluish tinge, as it flickered and danced over the walls of the cave.

It was going out! The oil must be exhausted; it would be a matter of minutes until darkness seeped over the cave!

Anne fixed her gaze on the dying light. It was dying like she would be soon, locked into a black tomb with no food or water. How long would it be? A few days at most. Or perhaps a week? The sea crashed against the rocks outside, yet without a source of fresh water, there could be no tomorrow.

The oil lamp shot sparks for a few seconds and then the wick extinguished itself. Darkness enveloped the cave like soft velvet. Anne put her head down in despair; she felt the spectre of death in this place. Even if someone should miss her at Islamorada, they would never think of looking here. Not at the place where Edward had died. Edward. She would be joining him soon. Anne closed her eyes tight; her twin seemed to be standing right here as he had so often in her past life.

Oh, Annie! There has to be a way out! How can you be so dense? Someone brought you into the place. If this someone is hiding something in the cave, there must be a way to leave and get out. Use your head! You can swim away, scuba tank or not! The Devil's Vortex will

197

carry you out, just as it carried me in years ago. Make like a camel and hoard up air in your lungs instead of water! You can do it! Besides, you have to capture the person responsible for this and you can't do it if you die buried in a cave underground!

Strange, how even the thought of Edward's voice could galvanize her into action. Anne opened her eyes; the all-enveloping darkness didn't appear quite as black. Or perhaps her eyes had adjusted to the gloom. The chinks and pinnacles of the dome of the cave let in orphaned, filtered shadows of the sun. And as Edward had said, someone had dragged her into the cave, so there had to be an entrance, somewhere, perhaps even underwater.

Anne crawled forward on her hands and knees. The floor seemed as solid as the rock surrounding it until she reached the two boxes set on the far side. As she scrambled upright and gave them a violent shove, she saw the watery, serpent-like hole leading downward.

It reminded her of Jonas in the *Bible*, looking into the mouth of a whale before being swallowed alive. He had survived his adventure and so would she! To find...

The answer. The answer which would lead to the person behind the murders at Islamorada, to the one who plotted her death now. If she escaped, she could go on to uncover the person responsible. If only...Anne turned back to stare deeply into the dark, malevolent hole in the cave's floor.

The answer stared her in the face. Beneath the cave ran the passages that she and Edward had been exploring five years earlier. Anne sat back on her heels; if she exited the cave, but ran out of air before hitting the surface, she would drown. The currents flowed within the malignant hole; the vortex of water that had thrown her spinning

198

toward the shore years ago originated here. If the tide came in, the speed of the water could knock her unconscious before she cleared the cave's underwater mouth.

Anne looked back at her prison beneath the rocks. She had no choice; no Lochinvar in shining white armor was going to rescue her. Her enemy had left her to die; Anne knew she would have to get out on her own.

She leaned back, tried to relax the muscles in her body and slow the blood that pumped at a hysterical rate through her veins while she filled her lungs with stale air. Staring at the black hole, Anne vowed silently that if she survived and escaped from the cave, she would never again decrease her lung capacity by smoking. I must get out to trap this murderer before he kills someone else, and I can't do that if I die in this macabre hole! As the air from the cave enveloped her, her lungs swelled once, twice, and then she toppled through the hole into the black depths below.

Anne kicked frantically downward like a crazy woman being dragged to the guillotine, her hand trailing along the rock marking the cave's bottom. She arrowed forward, the water pressing down on her, seeking to entomb her alive. The tunnel angled downward; Anne felt her ears pop as even more of her air bubbled out of her mouth.

Then the air vanished into bubbles above her head and her lungs began to burn like a red hot poker had been jabbed inside. Anne could feel her strokes getting weaker; her arms stopped stroking and fluttered, like a bird who tries to fly and can't. She pushed ahead while her mind wandered insanely; why couldn't Dirk Pitt or Al Giordino from Clive Cussler's latest underwater epic magically appear? Complete with scuba tanks and breathing apparatus, naturally. She turned a corner in the blackness, her eyes seeing thousands of blurring spots in front of her. Suddenly it seemed like such a waste of time to try and escape; the cold had evaporated, leaving her feeling so tired. Anne felt her strength vanish, leaving her exhausted and wanting only to stop and rest and sleep – to sleep forever. And Anne, in that moment, knew that she wasn't going to make it.

As she turned another corner, her body was lifted by a gigantic force and hurled forward, straight down the cave's corridor leading to the surface. She somersaulted over and around as the two tides slammed together within the narrow space in the passage, before retreating and vomiting her body out and upward. Anne's head snapped back; the pain returned her to consciousness as the vortex of spinning, swirling foam shoved past the waves and tossed her body, rag-like, onto the rocky outcropping of beach right below Islamorada.

Anne closed her eyes and tried to catch her breath as the phantoms from the blackness in the cave faded, to be replaced by the wind streaking across the water and blowing pieces of shale into her face. She coughed violently and scrubbed at her reddened eyes before slowly dragging herself erect. The storm had gotten worse during her sojourn in the cave; the weather seemed to have presented Key West with a possible hurricane. She needed to get back to Islamorada and soon, before the wind changed and tore her apart.

The rain started, gusting in from the southwest, as Anne tried to hurry. She had to get inside of Gordon Hall before the worst of the storm hit.

The first step once she reached home would be to report what had happened to the authorities. Stryker could discover who had been involved with the mysterious boxes in the cave and what had been smuggled there, besides catching the murderer, since the two were definitely linked in her mind.

The house came into view. Thinking it over, Anne decided that walking along in plain sight might turn out to be too dangerous – far better to enter through the kitchen door and get to the nearest telephone. Then she could sit tight and wait for the police.

Nothing moved nearby, either in the rose garden or across the veranda. The place looked deserted; the house felt hollow. Anne hurried upstairs to the alcove to use the telephone; as she picked up the receiver, she heard a gasp of shock.

It was only Maud.

"Anne!" She looked sepulcher white and sick, and something else, as though she couldn't quite believe her eyes.

Anne glanced down. Her slacks and blouse were shredded in half-a-dozen places from climbing through the rocks, while her dark hair had been knotted into a damp tangle; it felt as filthy as the clothes on her back.

"I don't have time to explain it all, Maud. But somebody has been smuggling something from Islamorada. They tried to kill me – again. Because I got too close to finding out the truth."

The telephone line appeared dead; the coming hurricane had knocked out the power lines. Even her cell 'phone wouldn't work. It seemed fortunate that they still had light in the house.

"The smugglers are the ones that have been responsible for the murders. First to drive people away by encouraging the legend about the gold being cursed. When that didn't work, they came out into the open. They've made millions on their racket and didn't want their little deal to end. Not for Spanish treasure or anything else."

Anne threw the telephone down in disgust.

Then she heard the sharp little click. A twenty-two caliber Beretta appeared in Maud's hand.

Anne looked at her face; she should have felt satisfaction over having discovered the identity of one of the murderers. All she did feel was extreme shock.

Chapter Twenty-one

"All that glisters is not gold…
Gilded tombs do worms enfold."
Merchant of Venice (Shakespeare)

Anne had never associated her aunt with firearms of any sort and yet here stood Maud, pointing a gun, as though she knew exactly how to use it – which perhaps she did.

Maud circled her slowly, forcing Anne back toward the stairway. The gun wavered in her hand.

"You're alive! I can't believe it. After everything we tried. You are lucky, Anne. But then, you always were."

The woman's face contorted into a mask of pain. Anne trembled violently.

"Why do you hate me so? I never did anything to you. At least that I remember."

"Oh, not you, my dear. Your mother. She had it all – everything I wanted – money, looks, youth, popularity. I would have killed for some of the chances she had. No man ever looked twice at me, even after she turned them down. I couldn't even get one of her rejects for a husband. Peg-Leg Maud. That was me."

Maud's lips pulled back, but she didn't smile. "You look just like her, Anne. And I thought I was rid of her when she ran off and got married. But even then, it wasn't my turn. It's never been my turn to shine." She gave a half-sob. "And then David allowed you and Edward to come here over the summers. And I loved him as much as I hated you! Every time I saw you, I saw your mother, too. I was so very conscious of the enormous resemblance. Naturally, it did make plotting against you that much easier."

Maud moved an inch toward the stairway. Anne circled her, watching closely. She saw a small black shadow detach herself from the back of the hall and prowl ahead.

"Things had been going so well for us. I finally found something I could do, bad leg and all. But Tom Saunders wanted more and more money all the time. He'd been smuggling the drugs for years. I knew it couldn't go on. But then your grandfather decided to see you again and there was no way I could turn him against you. I'd done it before over Edward. I tried my best, but the old fool stayed adamant. He saw you and immediately disinherited me on top of everything else! After I'd worked here for nothing for so many years! Perhaps he'd suspected what I'd been doing all along, trying to poison him against you. It won't matter in the end." Her face grew thoughtful. "The estate will revert to me when you're gone. All those millions will be mine. It should have been mine all along."

Anne didn't have to ask where she'd be going. She realized that her aunt had passed over the border line between rational and irrational, sane and insane. Maud was no longer responsible for her actions, but had changed into a stranger.

"You killed my grandfather! You kept the medicine from him. And it killed him!"

"Oh, no dear. I gave him some medicine. Just not the right kind. Aspirin has a multitude of uses," she added brightly, cheerfully, as though talking about the weather. "It all worked out. But you, you're far more resilient and resourceful than either of us planned. You're here in spite of it all." She sighed. "If you want something done…"

Her words trailed off, leaving Anne with the feeling that she was the one going mad. Maud stated things so logically, as if her acts seemed a rational course of action. Looking at her, Anne could see her aunt had come completely unhinged.

Anne edged a bit closer, hoping for a try at the gun. But Maud noticed the movement and raised the weapon higher.

"So you see, dear, everything will be taken care of. Even you." She studied Anne's face with no regret in her eyes at all.

"I think there is going to have to be another accident. To you. In a way, I'm sorry. Almost sorry, that is. But you haven't asked about yourself. Aren't you at all interested?"

Anne watched her hand, holding the gun.

"Considering everything else you've done, you're going to have to kill me, too. I can't be allowed to talk about the drugs and all."

"Yes. Although the smuggling is over, after tonight that is. The police are too close."

Anne moved a little farther to the left. She stood with her back to the wall, facing the staircase where Maud hovered. But poised on the top step directly behind the older woman was a small shadow with her slinky black tail. Jezebella had been crouched by the side of the step, her paws curled under her, hiding. Now she poked her head up and eased over onto the first stair.

Maud continued speaking. "It has to be. Surely you can see that. If you hadn't done so much snooping, it might not be necessary. Why didn't you just leave again and stay away after visiting David? All of this wouldn't be happening. I tried to warn Devlin with those notes, but nobody paid much attention." She spoke wearily. "But then David made you his heir, too. Of all those millions. And everything changed."

One of the floorboards creaked below. Anne heard it distinctly – more importantly, so had Maud. Someone had come in through the front door! Her eyes flickered down to the lower level but the person remained completely hidden.

Jezebella, who now crouched behind the first stair, blended into the dark carpeting.

Another sound came from below; the gun wavered, first backward, then forward. Anne tensed. Half of Maud's attention had focused on the person still downstairs, but her eyes reverted to the gun and the woman automatically brandished the Beretta while stepping downward onto the first stair.

Her left foot hit Jezebella a glancing blow, throwing Maud off balance. Normally, it wouldn't have mattered; with both hands free, she could have held the banister. But her left leg was hard to maneuver and she seemed determined to cover Anne with the gun. As her leg slid out from under her, she screamed and fell backward.

Anne tried to move forward as Maud started to fall. She could only watch as her aunt's body spun downward in slow motion before it picked up speed and crashed into the banister half-way down. She lay there in a black heap, arms spread, fingers splayed wide as though trying to catch something to stop her flight. Her back twisted at an odd angle and blood pumped out of her chest. The gun had disappeared.

Anne ran down the stairs, past Jezebella, who scurried in terror for the bedroom. Anne reached her aunt, knelt down and tried to stop the flow of blood.

A figure bounded up the stairs and slipped down by her side. Robin. The younger girl's face had turned the color of paste and her eyes seemed huge as she stared at Maud.

"I heard," Robin stuttered. "I heard what she said."

Maud groaned and Anne turned her attention back to her aunt. Maud's lips moved and she leaned closer.

"The *Riga,*" the older woman muttered. "On the *Riga!*"

"Who, Maud? Your partner? You said 'we' before. Who is it?"

Maud smiled, a sickly, hate-filled smile. Then her chest crackled and she coughed up some blood.

"Who do you think?" Her hand moved slowly to her arm, hovered, and tore back the sleeve. A golden encrusted identification bracelet appeared with the name "Edward" engraved on top.

Anne stared in disbelief. "No! It can't be! I don't believe it can be! Edward wouldn't be a part of this! Never!"

"He wouldn't take the bracelet off, Anne. You know that! Except to give it to me. You know his body was never found and Edward didn't die! He wants to meet you there. On the *Riga.*" Maud's breath hissed through her teeth. Blood ran from a corner of her mouth. "It's your destiny. And his...I...I hope..."

207

Her chest stopped moving. Maud's face froze in a nasty grimace, as though dying really didn't agree with her anymore than living had done.

Anne leaned back, Robin by her side.

"Where are the police? And Alex Stryker? They should be here!"

Robin stared transfixed at Maud, as though she couldn't look away.

"On the beach. They're all on the beach or in the woods. Lieutenant Stryker turned up, claiming he had new evidence and had to talk to you. That you were in grave danger. So everyone started hunting. Nobody could remember having seen you! One of them, I'm not sure who, found your shoes down on the beach. So everybody went out to search. The Lieutenant insisted on it. He paired us up. We've been scouring the estate for the last hour! We thought," and here she paused and licked her lips, "we thought you'd drowned!"

"Well, go down there. Tell them what's happened and to get out to the *Riga*. The murderer is on board!" Anne reached the front door and shouted back, "Move Robin. Go find the others. It's Edward that's out on that boat!"

She paused and then turned back to Maud, sprawled like a black angel of death on the floor. Anne reached down and pulled the golden identification bracelet from her arm.

"And tell Devlin," she continued, "to radio the Coast Guard to come out to the dive site as rapidly as possible!"

Robin's face mirrored her confusion.

"But where are you going?"

"The *Riga.* I've got to make it out there. I must talk to Edward. He might give himself up!" She turned and bolted again for the front door.

"But you can't! The storm. It's going to hit the coast in a few hours! You'll never make it!" Robin's voice rose to a shriek.

As the wind tore the door from the hinges, Anne almost agreed with her. But Edward remained on the dive ship and she really had no choice. Her twin, her other self. Blame from the past five years seeped anew into her soul. Anne couldn't, wouldn't just leave Edward to die. Not again. Never.

>>>>Gordon<<<<

Alex Stryker turned and watched as Robin Gordon bolted out of Islamorada and charged down toward the beach. Her light brown hair billowed out almost like a curtain in the rapidly rising wind under a black, soot-splotched sky that reminded him of a cauldron overturned.

"Alex," She halted, out of breath. "It's Anne! I saw her up at the house!"

Stryker felt his heart, which had been slamming into his rib cage for the last hour, slow at the news that Anne was alive. After finding her shoes on the beach, he had thought the worst, had thought...

His attention focused back on Robin.

"Tell me everything. And don't leave any part out!" he ordered calmly.

His brows knit as Robin poured out the story.

"So Maud Gordon told Anne that Edward is alive? And that he is responsible for the murders?"

"Yes. And Anne went out to the *Riga,* to try and get him to surrender, I think."

209

Stryker muttered angrily under his breath and turned to Armando Catalano, who had just come up.

"Get a Coast Guard boat over here now. We need to go out to the *Riga* right away. Anne Gordon is in deadly danger. And get Roger Devlin. He knows more about that dive boat than any other living soul. We may need his help, especially…" his gaze flew to the darkening clouds, "with the hurricane coming in."

Catalano hurried off to attend to Stryker's biding.

"But Edward would never hurt Anne! They were so close, their being twins and all. I was just a child, but I remember how much they cared about each other." Robin shoved her wind-tossed hair back from a very earnest face.

Stryker's gray eyes went hard as agate. "But that's the problem. It's not Edward Gordon who is on the *Riga*. It's someone…who wants nothing more than to see Anne dead!"

Chapter Twenty-two

"The power of the night, the press of the storm,
the post of the foe; where he stands,
the Arch Fear in a visible form;
yet the strong man must go."

Prospice (Robert Browning)

The sky turned ugly, shot through with black, streaked in molten gray. The cumulus-nimbus clouds hovered above as Anne reached the wharf and spotted the whaler tied up and waiting. Casting off the ropes, she started the outboard and aimed the small boat toward the *Riga.* The rain hit then, coming down in torrential sheets as the sea changed to a frothy white, plummeting the whaler around like a top gone berserk. Despite everything, Anne made progress, slow but sure, away from the relative safety of Islamorada on the shore and toward the dive boat where the murderer waited out the storm.

Anne ignored the elements as the small boat continued to bob and curvet like a cork in a bottle. She knew that Maud had never been agile enough, young enough, or good enough at scuba to have killed the divers, planted the snake in the Volkswagen and tried to kill her in the cave. It had to be somebody else. And if it turned out to be Edward? Could he have possibly survived the tragic accident in the cave five years ago? Anne clutched

211

the bracelet on her arm. She needed to know for her own peace of mind.

Anne scanned the horizon, hoping for a glimpse of the *Riga.* The waves and rain played havoc with the whaler; Anne shivered as the cold water pounded from all angles. The boat spun around as another large wave smacked it sideways, but miraculously, it straightened, pointed in the right direction, straight out to sea.

The waves threaded their way into the side of the boat, reaching out like angry serpents from the deep, curling their white fingers over the whaler at every toss. The spray tore at Anne while the water whirlpooled around her, an angry maelstrom, a devil's vortex of fury. It felt like the sea demons were actually rising from the boiling, bubbling cauldron below.

Anne paused and stared at the frothy foam for a long moment; it looked like the water could have given the storm on the Sea of Galilee serious competition. But nobody would miraculously appear and calm the waves and the turbulent tide. She'd just have to keep going and pray that the whaler didn't capsize before she reached the dive boat, *Riga.*

The shore line disappeared from view as the ocean seethed and tore from below while the rain beat pitilessly from above. The waves seemed to be attacking with greater force as Anne tried to keep the boat as steady as possible, hoping that it wouldn't fill up too fast and sink.

She had the strangest sensation of being alone on the sea; the land behind vanished, sucked up by the grayish mist that floated down. It reminded her of a kind of ghostly shroud, perhaps something painted by Albert Dore for the *Rime of the Ancient Mariner.* At least Anne didn't have an albatross hung around her neck, which was the only thing that could be said in her favor. As the ocean tore at the whaler with claw-like fingers, she looked ahead and spotted the black shape, looming up out of nowhere; the *Riga,* much nearer to shore. The storm seemed to have pushed her inland, far closer to the reef than earlier.

Anne searched the decks, but the dive boat looked deserted. Well, what did she expect? The murderer would hardly be waving a flag of welcome; Anne had been written off a number of hours before in the cave. She drew the whaler toward the old minesweeper, grasping the ladder hanging off the bow. As she and the little boat parted company, Anne dragged herself upward, over the gunwale of the ship and collapsed in a heap on the deck.

The rain plummeted down in sheets of steely gray. Finally, Anne raised her head.

The *Riga* seemed like a ghost ship, with no life on board whatsoever. Perhaps Maud had lied; perhaps nobody had been crazy enough to be on board in a near hurricane. But no, she had told the truth. The murderer waited and watched her like before. Anne could feel her skin crawl as waves of hate and animosity washed over her from an unseen, malevolent source.

She tried to scramble to her feet, but the boat corkscrewed heavily to the left, forcing her to drag herself upright, one inch at a time. The storm caused the *Riga* to heave and buck, violently like a wild thing against the sea. Anne slid across the lower deck on the starboard side, yanked open the companionway door and scrambled inside.

A second later she moved toward the bow of the *Riga.* She would begin searching on the bridge. It seemed a logical place that someone would go in weather like

213

this; although logic might not enter into it at this stage. Anne clambered up a series of accommodation ladders, only to be disappointed. The bridge appeared deserted.

She stopped to catch her breath. Dozens of places, no hundreds remained where someone might be hidden including the cabins, the dining room, galley, lounge, treasure room or drawing room lounge just for a start. Below deck was the engine room and the floating laboratory aft that Devlin had been so proud of, a specialty of the *Riga*. As Anne searched carefully, everything seemed to be completely devoid of life.

She perspired heavily, although her exertions hadn't been that great. The wind shrieked eerily outside, wailing like someone who mourned the dead. Finally Anne halted; she had been over the dive boat from the forepeak to the afterdeck. Only the engine room remained to be searched.

Anne slithered down another series of ladders into the bowels of the ship. The diesels had quieted; the whole place seemed too quiet. The elements beat against the *Riga* above deck but here, it felt calmer. She trudged past the treasure room, where the items from the *San Pedro* had been stored. The engine room glowed in semi-light. Anne didn't feel familiar with the place, despite Devlin and his tour of the minesweeper. She had Edward's bracelet fastened on her wrist; she ran her hand over it now, for courage. Then she stepped into the room and climbed down another ladder.

The place stank of oil and burning fuel; the *Riga's* engines had been disabled by the storm. Anne moved farther into the room to peer at a pipe with water gushing out. Then the door creaked ominously closed behind her;

she turned slowly and saw the gun held in a steady hand –
a thirty-two caliber revolver.

"How nice of you to join me, Anne. And with all
the rotten weather, yet."

And Cristel Slivka laughed hollowly, her white
teeth glinting in a wolf-like smile in the half light.

>>>>*Gordon*<<<<

Anne faced Cristel Slivka, her business partner from
Cedar Key, her mind in turmoil. The drug smuggler
turned murderer laughed again.

"I know you, Anne. I knew you would be along.
You have to be involved. I've been watching you for so
long, working as a diver on the *Riga*. I left Cedar Key and
followed you down here, landed a job and voila! Here I
am! Devlin is desperate for help with the salvage
operation. All divers look alike in those black scuba suits
and it made keeping tabs on you and Stryker so much
easier! Devlin is such a sad, trusting fool. I had complete
access to Islamorada." She shook her head slowly.
"Well, now you can relax. You're going down with the
ship, so to speak, while I," and here Cristel dangled the
key to the treasure room in front of Anne, "am going to
escape with the loot and live happily ever after."

Anne felt the bracelet move on her wrist. "And
Edward?"

"Little snot-nosed Edward? Is that how Maud got
you out here? My dear mother? Edward is dead! Dead,
do you hear? I was there that day, watching you. And
Edward washed up, farther down the coast. But he wasn't
dead. Not then. I took the bracelet off of his body myself
after I crushed his head with a rock. I dragged Edward
back into the vortex and the current running past

215

Islamorada pulled him out to sea. He's gone, Anne. He can't help you anymore."

Anne felt her world tipping crazily on its axis. Edward had been alive and Crystal had killed him! She licked suddenly dry lips and tried to concentrate on what else the woman had said. "Maud was your mother?"

"Oh, yes. Mother dearest. And can you guess who my father was?"

Anne's mind clicked. "Saunders? Tom Saunders?"

"Very good, Anne. Daddy was good old reliable Saunders. He met Maud one night. And I...I was Maud's little mistake twenty-five years ago. Tom Saunders wanted to marry her; I'll say that for him. They were going to run off together. Kind of like your mother and Devon Sharp and you and Leigh. Maybe it runs in the family!" Cristel cackled with hysterical laughter before she continued. "Everything might have been fine except your grandfather found out. He wanted Maud to get rid of the problem. Paid Saunders off so he wouldn't interfere. Of course Daddy knuckled under. But Maud decided to have the child and went to Europe, somewhere, at a spa for unwed mothers in Switzerland. After six months, there I was! But my dear mother decided she couldn't keep me. So she farmed me out to a family in Key West." The gun in her hand trembled slightly. "Need I say that Joan Crawford didn't have anything on that bunch. Maud used to come visit when she could get away from the old man. Everyone stayed all smiles until she left. Anyway, one time I followed her home. To Islamorada. I slipped under the back fence. They had given a party for you and your twin with a pony to ride and presents and a huge cake. I watched from behind one of the rhododendron bushes. Finally the gardener saw me and chased me out."

"I think I remember!" Anne mused quietly. "The party, I mean. But we never knew! Edward and I, we never knew!"

Cristel Slivka went on as though she hadn't heard, as though she lived in a time years ago. "It was one of many parties. I used to sneak back and watch and wait. I explored the estate, too. The tree house, the wharf…"

"But why didn't you tell us? We could have…"

"Could have what? Maud acted ashamed of me while your precious grandfather worried about the family name being disgraced. But then…, then everything changed."

"How?" Anne murmured, although she thought she knew.

"Edward died. And Maud realized that you would inherit Islamorada when David Gordon passed on. She hated you! Did you even realize it? Of course, I hated you too, like I've never hated another human being in my life. You and Edward both. All that money and I didn't have a cent to call my own. Although Edward might have taken care of my dear Mommy provided he never found out about the drug business she had been running."

"And I would have helped you, too!"

"No, Anne, you are just too Puritan, like your grandfather. All those kids, looking for a fix. I just gave them what they wanted and supplied one. But you wouldn't have seen it that way."

Anne remained silent as Cristel continued.

"Those miserable little nothings, destroyed because of the dope. They would have ruined their lives anyway! With or without the drugs. Saunders smuggled the dope to New York, mainly. It's where I'm from if you remember and it's where Leigh and I first met. Only he

217

wasn't smart enough to be a smuggler or much of anything else remotely useful. And then he met and married you and got cut off completely from Islamorada." She sighed dramatically. "What a dolt!"

"You said Maud needed you?" Anne thought of the woman lying dead on the stairway at Islamorada. Cristel wouldn't know about it and she wasn't going to tell her.

"Of course! As a spy! She needed someone to keep track of you since her brother willed you Islamorada. And Mommy couldn't do it with the gimpy leg of hers. Originally, she just wanted to discredit you with the old man. And you made it so easy."

"With Leigh." It wasn't a question.

"Yes. Leigh Giddings. I knew he'd be exactly the kind of worthless, low-life of a nothing that would appeal to you. What a bone-headed, money grubbing fool! Leigh thought you would get Islamorada, but then he ruined your chances with that marriage and divorce. Fifty million dollars! No wonder you came running back when your grandfather beckoned! And that blockhead Giddings ruined everything!"

"But what was the big secret? What was worth the fifty thousand dollars that Leigh wanted?"

"The fool saw me taking the drugs from the tree house. And he started to put things together. He cornered me and threatened to talk to you and the police about me and Mommy dearest and Saunders unless we cut him in! We would have gone to jail! I couldn't have that. So Leigh had to die."

Cristel Slivka shifted her position as the boat rose and fell under them.

"I think it's getting a little worse out. We don't have much time. I have work to do – moving some of the treasure for one thing."

"That's why you came out here? To collect treasure?"

"I thought you'd died, Anne. I wanted you to die slowly in the cave. Starving is so unpleasant. I know from personal experience when I lived with my charming foster family in Key West. I'd almost killed you with the snake, but you got away." She sighed. "Try, try again, I suppose."

"You really hated me that much?"

"You had everything I'd always wanted! And thrown it all away! I loathed you!"

"And Tom Saunders? He's your father, Cristel. And you followed me to Orlando, met him and then killed him by staging an accident in his shower?"

"Another fool and so trusting! They all were! He didn't have any stomach for murder, just drug smuggling! Got cold feet and threatened to tell you what was going on when you came to Orlando. Not for money. He developed a conscience! He didn't mind collecting money for the drugs. He just didn't want to get too dirty with a few murders."

"A few murders? Those divers on the boat? That was you then?"

"I had to scare them away, didn't I? They ruined our drug hideout, salvaging that stupid Spanish galleon. I came down here to work from Cedar Key on and off, usually when you thought I was away taking pictures and got myself hired out on the dive boat. I'd learned how to scuba when I was a kid living on the Keys, only the accidents kind of got out of hand and turned into murder.

219

It wasn't really my fault. I pretty much had to handle things on the *Riga* myself. Just like," and here her voice dropped, "I'm going to have to handle you now."

Anne stared at the gun in her hand and knew she had only seconds to live. Cristel Slivka had talked herself out and nothing more remained to be said.

Cristel continued speaking, her eyes black-pitted pools of hate as she watched Anne cringing up against the far wall. "Actually, this has worked out rather well. You will go over the side, lost at sea, and the treasure will mysteriously vanish. All I need do is get in the dinghy with my loot and disappear. Who will ever know that you didn't drown at sea? Your body may never even be recovered. Down to the depths with poor Edward in the Devil's Vortex." The woman spat the last name out.

"What do you want, Cristel? Money?"

A harsh laugh answered her.

"I have more than enough, thank you! No, I need you dead, Anne. Dead and permanently quiet. I'm going to be sure this time. We're going to take a walk up on deck and you're going over the side." She gestured with the gun. "So get moving."

Anne turned slowly, her hands raised, backing away. No little black cat would appear to help her this time. And Cristel Slivka seemed to know how to shoot as well as how to sail and scuba dive.

Anne backed farther until she finally reached the accommodation ladder. It dug into her back as Cristel waved the gun menacingly.

"Climb!" she ordered calmly.

Then the pipe that had been hissing and leaking when Anne first entered the engine room let loose with a loud pop, almost like a gunshot. Cristel spun around as a stream of water gushed out and hit her full in the back, giving Anne the chance she had been waiting for. As the gun went off, Anne bounded deer-like through the treasure room and down the companionway to disappear through the open doorway beyond.

Chapter Twenty-Three

"I was ever a fighter, so...one fight more,
the best and the last!"

Prospice (Robert Browning)

Anne peered around; she'd hidden in one of the diver's cabins and knew Cristel couldn't be far behind. She saw a bunk across the way; Anne hesitated and slid underneath to catch her breath.

Cristel's footsteps resounded outside moments later. She stopped and listened, trying to pick up a hint of Anne's location. Then her footfalls sounded as the woman walked to the port cabin. The wind blasted harder outside; over the racket of the storm was the commotion of Cristel Slivka creating havoc next door.

Anne slid out from under the bed, slipped to the door, cracked it open a bit and looked down the corridor. The companionway appeared empty. Anne picked up a heavy, and no doubt priceless, vase from the table and hurled it against the bulkhead; Cristel heard the crash and bounded out of the other cabin as planned. Turning, she dived toward the sound of the noise, running past the starboard cabin and up the passageway. Anne didn't falter, but scrambled from behind the door where she'd been watching and scurried for the stairs, not even glancing back.

As Anne climbed toward the deck above, she heard Cristel Slivka bellow in anger. The woman rushed back down the companionway and up the steps to follow as Anne ran for'ard into the salon and hid behind the sofa.

Anne waited. Cristel's footfalls rang clear as she moved past the salon and climbed the accommodation ladder to the wheelhouse above.

The minutes passed. Suddenly the *Riga* shuddered as though she had been skewed in half; the deck swayed violently. Anne fell sideways across the floor. The dive boat must have crashed into a part of the reef; it was the only explanation that made any kind of sense.

Anne scrambled up and squinted out of a porthole on the starboard side. Fingers of cobweb-gray mist seeped over everything and limited her vision, but she didn't need twenty-twenty eyesight to see the reef or the waves that shot phosphorescent streams of water high onto the *Riga's* bow. The boat bobbed skyward, turning at an impossible ninety-degree angle as the sea sought to tear the ship apart. Anne stared and the scene faded from sight as the vessel rocked back toward the port side.

The *Riga* felt adrift. Only minutes remained until the boat collided with the reef if it hadn't already done so; the dragging anchors had not been able to hold it in the hurricane seas. And when that happened, the vessel's insides would be torn out by the sharp corals and the *Riga* would sink like the proverbial rock.

Anne shut her eyes and leaned against the wall. Then she knew; someone watched her. As though on cue, Cristel spoke.

"So I've found you again. We must stop meeting like this. Someone might get the idea I actually like you!"

She had the gun pointed directly ahead. Strangely, Anne felt almost resigned; even if she should escape from

Cristel, nobody could escape from the *Riga* before the minesweeper came apart.

"What does anything matter Cristel? You can't get away! The ship is going to smash up under us! It's not going to be that much longer. We'll both end up dead!"

"I don't see things like you do. I think with my luck, the *Riga* might just last out the storm. I've been lucky this far. As usual."

"I wouldn't be too sure. You know how Devlin feels about the vessel. He'll be here as soon as the storm abates." And so would Alex Stryker – to find her. Dead.

"And I'll have vanished. With this, naturally." She held up a part of the treasure. "I couldn't carry it all. Too heavy. But this gold and jewelry plus the drug money will be enough for a fresh start after I pull out of Key West."

Anne had played the scene many times before. She eased back, but Cristel saw the movement and stopped her with a wave of the gun.

"Oh, no! Don't try it! You and I are going to walk up on deck. You're going to have a nasty fall overboard. In the storm, it won't be surprising."

Anne thought of the serpent sea below and the reef beyond. "Why don't you shoot me and have it over with?"

"But I couldn't do that. Suppose the body washed ashore with a bullet in it? That would be murder! Much easier to have you fall over the side. Saves me all kinds of unnecessary worry. And work."

"Cristel, it's no good. Too many people know what you've done. Can't you understand?"

Her mouth twisted in a savage line; she gestured with the gun.

"Walk down the companionway to the deck. Now!"

Anne considered providing a distraction as she opened the door leading to the deck. A barrage of wind and rain blew into her face. Then the situation miraculously changed.

The rain drenched Anne inside of two seconds. Cristel followed right behind, swaying as the deck rocked furiously. The water tore up under the hull and Anne heard a metallic screech as the *Riga* whirled to-and-fro. She swung to face Cristel away from the starboard guardrail, the torrential gusts of rain and water beating on her back.

"Cristel, listen to me! I can help you if you'll let me!"

"You, help me?" She seemed to find the idea amusing. "The only way you can help me now, Anne, is by dying." She motioned with the gun, for'ard, toward the bow of the dive ship as a turbulent gust of wind tore into her. Anne clutched at the guard railing and hung on for dear life.

Cristel seemed so close, the gun clutched in her hand while the deck heaved beneath the two of them. Anne still backed away, slipping and sliding on the foredeck. She turned suddenly above the fury of the storm, senselessly, perhaps, but she had to know.

"Were the drugs and murders worth it, Cristel? All the misery and agony?"

Cristel smiled, framing her words distinctly as though speaking to a child. Despite the clamor of the sea and sky, Anne heard her plainly.

"I've got more money in the bank than I'll ever spend. I'll have everything I ever wanted. Ponies and

225

birthday parties and tree houses or whatever. And nobody will ever look down on me again."

"Material things, Cristel. They won't make you happy." Anne thought again of Alex Stryker. He loved her! She loved him. And now...

"Who are you to say? You asked if it were worth it. It's been worth everything and more besides. And I wouldn't change a thing even if I could!"

They stood standing face to face at the rail. Cristel Slivka was so close that Anne could have touched her had she wanted to. The *Riga* continued to buck underneath them, being pulled apart like a small stick in the boiling cauldron on the sea.

"You just don't care, do you? About your father or my grandfather or even Leigh. You don't care about the people who have died or the misery you've caused."

"You missed your calling, Anne. You should have been a preacher instead of a photographer." The gun shifted slightly in her hand. "If you'll just step over to the rail. I want to be sure that the accident you're going to have is fatal. Nobody could live in a sea like this."

Anne could hear the determination in her voice; deliberation was written all over Cristel's face. Anne stepped slightly back, the water sluicing off her body, but she had nowhere to go and she knew it.

In that instant, the *Riga* rose high into the air, plunged down into the trough of an enormous wave and cracked once again into the coral reef. The ship shuddered as though she had received a mortal wound. The deck slipped beneath Cristel Slivka and Anne; they both heard a scraping sort of rumble as the bow plowed toward the bottom. The dive boat gave an ungainly lurch and Anne fell forward onto her knees, sliding over the

226

deck. The gun went off in Cristel's hand, but Anne didn't waste time wondering; she just scrambled to get as far from the sea as possible. Anne slammed against the outside cabin door with a sharp clunk; her head snapped downward and she remained only half-conscious as she saw Cristel sliding close by the rail.

The woman had managed to regain control of the gun for all the good it seemed to be doing her. The *Riga* swung toward the starboard side again, throwing Cristel back across the deck. She hit the guardrail, which gave an ugly crunch and splintered outward. Anne opened her mouth to shout a warning to no avail as Cristel plunged into the whirlpool of the ocean below. Anne dragged herself painfully over the deck, but the woman had vanished; nothing but the pounding waves remained, rising like white, sooty spirals into the air. The weight of the Spanish gold from the *San Pedro* had pulled Cristel down instantly.

Anne stared for a moment before dragging herself back to safety. The dive ship felt like it was going to come completely apart. Pulling upward, she sought the nearest doorway, but the vessel gave a last convulsive heave. Anne closed her eyes, shutting out the serpent sea all around her.

Then she turned suddenly and fell, hitting the deck hard. Her head smashed into a very solid, immovable object and she remembered nothing more.

>>>>*Gordon*<<<<

Stryker lifted the dark red blanket out of Roger Devlin's arms and wrapped it carefully around Anne Gordon's shoulders. Her breathing steadied. Finally, her lashes flickered and her eyes opened wide, staring, uncomprehending at the scene around her.

Stryker felt his heartbeat return to normal as Anne's eyes focused on him. Recognition flared in their depths .

"Where am I?" she finally mumbled.

Devlin answered the question. "We're aboard the Coast Guard cutter. When I heard from Robin that you and the murderer were on the *Riga*, I figured you'd need help. Alex and I got here right before my dive boat disintegrated on the reef. We managed to get to you just in time."

Alex passed Anne half of his cup of coffee; she sat up slowly and sipped at it.

"What happened to Cristel Slivka? She was the murderer and drug smuggler. She and Maud and Tom Saunders. They ran a smuggling ring out of Islamorada. That's why she killed the divers and sabotaged the treasure ship. To scare people and keep them away from finding out about their nasty little racket. And…she killed Edward five years ago. She admitted it to me!"

Stryker and Devlin exchanged a look. Finally Devlin spoke. "We searched the entire area but there was no sign of her. I think she actually did drown. Nobody could survive after going overboard in this kind of weather."

"No, I suppose not." Anne put the coffee cup carefully down. "Cristel Slivka killed so many people. And Maud helped, too."

"Don't think about it," Stryker put in. "What's done is done. There's no way we could have helped Maud, so perhaps this is for the best. This way there will be no trial. No publicity. Nothing."

"You're absolutely right. She would have never been prosecuted. Her mind went completely at the end." Anne searched Stryker's face. "What's going to happen?"

"Why, we're going back to shore and wait out the storm." Stryker smiled for the first time. "The drug smuggling business, at least at Islamorada, seems to have been shut down permanently. The murderer is drowned. There's nobody left for me to put in jail."

Devlin pulled himself erect and headed for the door. "I'd best see to the ship. We've got a ways to go before this weather blows over." With a backward wave, he vanished, closing the door firmly behind him.

Anne looked at Stryker for a long minute; then his arms folded around her.

"I thought you'd been killed. When Robin said you'd gone out to the ship because you thought Edward was alive...only I knew it wasn't Edward but Cristel Slivka. She was involved and likely the murderer."

"How did you know?"

"I told Armando Catalano to check into the histories of people at Islamorada. Just had a hunch. And then I discovered Maud had had a child twenty-five years ago in Switzerland. When I found out what had happened to Tom Saunders in Orlando and that you'd gone up there and possibly been followed, we started checking the airlines. One of the ticket agents remembered Cristel. She was strikingly good looking and the agent paid some attention. The clincher happened when the woman identified Cristel's photograph. She remembered her because of this ring on her third finger. A huge opal the agent said."

229

"Yes, an opal. I'd seen it many times." Realization dawned. "Cristel was…a Scorpio! And she was also my cousin!"

>>>>*Gordon*<<<<

"Anyway, once we knew she'd flown to Orlando, all the pieces started coming together. Tom must have called her and said that you were coming to talk. Cristel got cold feet about what her father was going to say. Drug smuggling is one thing. Murder is something else. And then we found out about her adoption by a foster family in Key West. It must have been pretty grim."

Stryker paused and continued. "I knew you were in danger so I rushed back to the estate, but you'd gone missing. And Robin found us searching the beach and told me about Maud and Edward and that you had gone out to the *Riga*. The storm had been cutting up the inlet for hours. Devlin called the Coast Guard, but I wasn't sure we'd be in time."

A knock sounded on the door and Devlin stuck his head around the corner.

"It will be awhile until we make it back. I told the police to have an ambulance waiting to take you to the emergency center, Anne. The medics will check you out. Everything will be fine. You'll see." With another wave and an encouraging smile, he vanished.

Anne leaned back, the red blanket wrapped tightly around her. Her hands shook uncontrollably and the tears welled in her eyes.

Alex Stryker watched her compassionately.

"Don't try and think too much about things, Anne. This all started a long time ago with a lot of mistakes other people made. But there's no reason for you to feel guilty – about Edward or anyone else. There was nothing you could have done. Remember that, if you don't remember anything else."

"You're right, Alex. There's nothing I could have done." Anne closed her eyes. "Nothing at all. And, it really is over."

"Everything except for you and me." Stryker's arms tightened around her once more and he tenderly kissed her cheek. "I don't plan for that to ever be over. I hope," he said with a laugh in his voice, "that it takes Devlin a good long while to get this boat to shore."

"You and me both."

Alex Stryker stared into her eyes dark with passion as his lips came down on hers. And he completely forgot about the rest of the world as he held Anne in his arms.

Epilogue

One month later.

> *"Healing is a matter of time,*
> *But it is sometimes also a matter of opportunity."*
>
> *Precepts* (Hippocrates)

"I now pronounce you man and wife." The Reverend Bassinger turned to the couple standing before him. "You may kiss the bride." He smiled at Alex Stryker as he enfolded Anne in his arms.

Everything has been just too perfect, Anne Gordon Stryker thought as she looked up into her husband's handsome face.

As they walked back down the aisle at the Islamorada Chapel, Anne caught Robin grinning happily at her in her light green bridesmaid dress. She tossed her bridal bouquet into the younger woman's hands before her new husband helped her into their car. Anne saw Robin turn into Ben Caldwell's arms; watching the two together, Anne had a feeling they would soon be celebrating another wedding at Islamorada.

Alex drove quickly north on Route 1 toward Miami. He glanced sideways at Anne's face. "What are you thinking, my love? You've been so quiet."

Anne roused herself. "I was wishing that my grandfather had still been here for the wedding. But perhaps…he knows that we got married and can see how happy I am."

Alex maneuvered their car around a slow-moving truck.

"I'm sure he does know. Somehow, I think he knows all of it. Your grandfather always could keep tabs on everyone while he was living. He's probably doing the same right now. And you said our honeymoon spot at Glitter Bay in Barbados was where he and his wife stayed years ago."

"I think he would approve of our choice, Alex. And of everything else that's happened in the last few weeks."

Alex glanced sideways and saw the shadow cross her face.

"Are you still having the nightmares?"

"Sometimes. And I can almost feel the deck of the *Riga* moving under me in the hurricane. Although…I'm free in a way. Free from the blame of Edward's death. From the moment Crystal admitted what she had done. And I had my grandfather's forgiveness, too. I'm free from all the memories that haunted me at Islamorada."

"You don't have to worry any more. I'm here and I can handle any problem you may have. Although…"

"Yes," Anne smiled contentedly. "It's marvelous the way everyone rallied around. Colin will be taking care of Islamorada and my grandfather's business until we return from Barbados, and he'll run things while we're in Miami because of your job. He even volunteered to take care of Jezebella when Robin's not at the estate."

"And the movie company has moved on, thank goodness. Roger Devlin lost everything when the Riga smashed up on the reef. All that gold scattered over the ocean floor that was waiting to be transferred is gone."

Stryker shook his head slowly. "Who could know that the hurricane would be the worst in years?"

"I heard that Devlin moved his salvage operation over to Matecumbe Key. And Peter James, Aldridge and Frank Blaine are all back in Hollywood. The script idea for the *San Pedro* got shelved and P.J. is supposed to be working on a Dracula movie." Anne paused before continuing. "All the time they spent here. The only thing good to come of it is Aldridge's marriage to Diana Moon. I hope they have their happily ever after ending."

Stryker reached over to grasp her hand. "If they don't, I know we will."

A short silence followed before he continued. "It was generous of you to have Maud buried next to your grandfather, Anne."

"She wasn't responsible, Alex. I think her mind went completely at the end. And it's what she would have wanted. As for Crystel," Anne stopped and continued more slowly, "Cristel's body wasn't recovered. The divers think the hurricane dragged her out to sea. I still can't believe it! Everything she did to me." Anne paused and bit her lip before turning to Stryker. "But I found you, so it was all worth it." She hesitated. "For a while, I thought you had done it, you know. I thought you'd been involved with everything that had happened at Islamorada."

"Well, I thought that you had done it, too. Especially when Tom Saunders died and you admitted to having gone to Orlando to see him. I'm so very glad," he murmured softly, "that we both thought wrong!"

And he smiled at Anne, lovingly, before he piloted the car through the gate leading to Miami's International Airport.

Other Books by Linda Masek

Mag-ni-fi-cat
The Poison Tree
Soul Dance

Other Books by Fireside Publications

Dreams ~ Shadows of the Night by Olivia Claire High

Odds & Ends* Bits & Pieces by Joye O'Keefe

Beyond Forever: Past Life Experiences by Taylor Shaye

Deadly Visions by Lois Wilmoth-Bennett (Kindle)

Essays: On Living with Alzheimer's Disease: The First Twelve Months by Lois Wilmoth-Bennett

The Find by James J. Valko

Amanda's Voice by Eileen Bennett (True Crime)

Ice Rose by Alison Neuman (YA Spy Novel)

Independence Day Plague by Carla Lee Suson

For more information on these and other Fireside books, please visit:

www.Firesidepubs.com or
http://kadinbooks.com
Also available on Amazon.com and Kindle